The Heavy Crown
Reaper Bastards MC, Washington, D.C. Chapter
Linny Lawless

Contents

Cover Models: Boomer Paschall

Photography: Jean Woodfin, JW Photography

Cover Design: Linny Lawless

Editing and Proofreading: Mitzi Carroll and Marisa Nichols

Personal Assistants: Mikki Thomas and Kristin Youngblood

Heavy, the President of the Washington DC chapter of the Reaper Bastards MC reigns as the King in a dirty city of porn, money, and blood.

Heavy saved my life seven years ago and told me to never return. He was my shield, my rock, with dark grey eyes that burned through me. Now I've walked right back into Heavy's world to see the hatred and rage in his eyes. But he cannot hide the sensual hunger and feral desire to own my heart, dominate my body, and possess my soul – a silent promise I'll belong to him no matter the cost and no one will get in his way.

SONG LIST

BLACK LABEL SOCIETY – Grimmest Hits Album

Trampled Down Below

Seasons of Falter

The Betrayal

All That Once Shined

The Only Words

Room of Nightmares

A Love Unreal

Disbelief

The Day That Heaven Had Gone Away

Illusions of Peace

Bury Your Sorrow

Nothing Left to Say

Buckcherry

LIT UP

For the Movies

Ridin'

Sorry

Next 2 You

Everything

Crazy Bitch

Rescue Me

Rose

All Night Long
Gluttony
Nothing Left but Tears

"Uneasy lies the head that wears a crown."
William Shakespeare

PART 1
7 YEARS AGO

CHAPTER 1
DANIKA

REAPER BASTARDS

 MC

WASHINGTON, D.C.

It was the night of my eighteenth birthday, and I was finally free. I climbed out of my bedroom window and ran away, vowing to myself that no matter how bad it ever got, I would never go back to that house. My mom and dad would come home when the sun was just rising to find me gone...again. I'd done it a dozen times before. The horrible and sick memories of what happened in that house would always stay with me. I hoped that those memories would fade over the years and feel they belonged to someone other than me. I was on my way to see Krista Miller, the only friend I had from high school. Her parents were college-educated, white-collar business types that made a whole ton of money. They lived in a big house in a nice neighborhood, across the railroad tracks from the shitty trailer park I lived in. But Krista, like her younger brother,

Nathan, didn't care about living in a nice neighborhood. They entertained themselves by smoking weed, crystal meth, and even snorted coke if they could get it.

I stuffed a thick roll of cash in my jeans pocket. It was five hundred dollars that I saved up working at the consignment shop. It was all the money I had to get away from my parents and that house. I had my burner phone in my jacket pocket and carried a backpack with some clothes, a hairbrush, and a toothbrush. I walked for about a mile south, wearing a gray hoodie, jeans, and my purple chucks I bought from the consignment shop. I pulled my hair back in a ponytail and wore a baseball cap. That way, I looked more like some vagrant or a homeless person walking down Route 1 in the dark. I made it to Krista's house and climbed into the basement window to find her sniffling and rubbing her nose. I didn't like seeing Krista do drugs, and I hoped that it was just a phase she was going through to anger her stuck-up parents.

When all the girls talked about boys and dating, I made my education my number one priority. I knew boys wouldn't help me get a high school diploma—that was all on me. I was such a recluse in school—keeping to myself—and didn't make friends easily. I was ashamed of myself and kept all the terrible things that were happening to me deep down inside. I hid it well and stayed invisible to everyone in school, dressing in plain and unnoticeable T-shirts and jeans. I bought my own clothes at the consignment shop since my parents spent any money they had on liquor and weed.

Krista squealed, wrapping her arms around my neck before I could drop my backpack on her couch. "Happy birthday, Dani!" She planted a kiss on my cheek.

I hugged her back, squeezing my eyes shut, hoping not to cry. "I'm eighteen and free to do whatever the fuck I want!"

Krista pulled back—her eyes all glassy. "We're going to celebrate tonight like two bad-ass *be-otches*! I have a surprise!"

I dropped my pack on her couch, sitting down next to it and groaned. "I don't like surprises, Krista. You know that."

"I know, but I couldn't tell you the surprise until I found out if it was going to really happen."

"What is it, Krista!?"

She jutted out her hip, "You remember Tye, right?"

I had a sinking feeling in the pit of my stomach. "Yeah, I remember him. He doesn't have any teeth. Isn't he like fifty years old?"

She huffed. "No, silly. He's thirty-one! The Reaper Bastards are patching-in a prospect and throwing a crazy-as-fuck party tonight!"

I arched my brow. "What's a patching-in?"

"The guys start out as a prospect, and when they get patched-in, they become members and celebrate by throwing a kick-ass party! It's a big deal with diamond clubs. Tye told me today that you and I are invited!"

I didn't really know much about motorcycle clubs, only from what Krista told me. Whenever I saw a biker wearing a vest with patches on it, I feared them. And the women that rode with them were just as intimidating.

"Don't you think that's a little strange?" I asked, rummaging in my backpack. I pulled out a half-empty bottle of cheap vodka, twisted the cap off, tilted it up, and took a shot. I squeezed my eyes shut and pursed my lips. It tasted like rubbing alcohol.

I handed the bottle to Krista. "I've been fucking Tye now for a few months, Dani. He's got some good weed and some great crystal. We can't pass this up! It's not easy to get into one of these parties. I know for sure the Reaper Bastards throw a fucking hell of a party compared to those stupid jock parties with the prissy bitches and dumbass football players." She took a shot of the vodka and puckered her lips at the aftertaste. "Let's make your eighteenth birthday memorable. This MC party will be one you'll never forget!"

I slung my backpack on and followed Krista back out the basement window. We walked down the street together, as I carried the bottle of vodka inside my hoodie jacket. We stood at the corner of Krista's street about ten houses away from hers when a black Ford van pulled up alongside the curb. Krista grabbed my hand, opened the passenger door, and climbed in first. I jumped in after as she slid across the bench seat next to Tye.

He grinned, and even though it was dark, I could see that he was missing another tooth. He wore jeans and a black T-shirt, but he wasn't wearing his Reaper Bastards vest like he did when I met him the first time. "Hey, you sexy little thang."

Krista leaned into him. "Hey, Tye." Then she kissed him.

I felt like puking but took another shot of vodka.

Tye leaned over and looked at me. "Krista tells me it's your birthday, darlin'?"

I met his eyes. "My name is Danika, not darlin'. And yeah, it's my birthday."

I gasped when Tye reached over, grabbing the sleeve of my hoodie. "You better be careful how you talk to me, bitch. You say somethin' snotty, and you'll get a fist up your tight ass." He shoved me back, and my head bumped the passenger window.

"She's just nervous, Tye! She's never been to a patch-in party," Krista said as she hugged him, trying to calm him down.

I straightened up in the passenger seat and took another shot of vodka as Tye stomped on the gas.

Tye parked the van in front of a bar in Washington DC called the Dirty Rooster Saloon. The street lights in the parking lot illuminated two rows of motorcycles parked side by side. I left my backpack and the almost empty bottle of vodka in the van. Since Krista insisted on it, I left the baseball cap too. When we climbed out, Tye wrapped an arm around Krista then squeezed her ass while I followed behind them. I kept my head down but looked over at the parked motorcycles and the two men who stood by them. They had leather vests on, with only one patch on the back along the bottom that read *Prospect*.

There was a big guy covered in tattoos standing out front of the bar checking IDs. Both Krista and I had fakes, but since we were with Tye, I figured we wouldn't need them since the big guy just let us walk right in. The mechanical bull in the center of the bar was the first thing that caught my attention as I followed Krista and Tye to the bar. I saw a few men wearing the Reaper Bastard vests and women barely dressed in mini-skirts, shorts, fishnets. It was definitely a biker bar with two stripper poles on either end of the long bar. Heavy metal music blared loudly, and the whole place was dimly lit. Clouds of smoke and the scent of cigarettes, cigars, and weed wafted through the air.

Tye walked up to the bar, waving down a girl dressed in a black bikini to serve us drinks. Commotion and whistles came from the other end of the bar. A blonde woman, dressed in a black skin-tight bodysuit, was hauled up onto the bar by one of the bikers. I watched, making sure my jaw didn't drop as she began to dance around one of the poles. More bikers gathered around and began to holler and whistle when Krista turned around and handed me a bottle of beer.

I tilted the bottle, taking several gulps until it was already half empty. My eyes landed on the man wearing a Reaper Bastards vest staring in my direction. It was dark in the bar, but I could tell his arms were covered in tattoos. He was tall, with broad shoulders, dark hair like mine, and a full beard. He looked angry and glared. I looked behind me, hoping he was glaring at someone else and not me. But there was no one there. I felt my face flush, and I swallowed the lump in my throat, feeling a bit intimated when I turned back.

I blinked and suddenly looked down when he began to saunter toward me. Tye wrapped an arm around me then, pulling me up against his side.

The tall, dark-haired man approached and was now glaring at Tye. "This is a private party, Tye. Only club members and sweetbutts allowed," he barked, his deep voice loud over the metal music.

Tye pulled me closer to his side and chuckled. "It's cool, Heavy. They're both sweetbutts. And they're mine."

I gritted my teeth and wanted to bust my beer bottle over the top of Tye's head just then. I shoved him off me. "I'm not your fucking sweetbutt!"

"Didn't I tell you not to talk shit, you little bitch!" Krista cried out when Tye raised his hand to hit me.

I flinched, but the man called Heavy grabbed Tye's wrist, blocking him. "Fuck off; she's not your sweetbutt. She's *mine*."

CHAPTER 2
HEAVY

REAPER BASTARDS

MC

WASHINGTON, D.C.

The patch-in party for Wrecker at the Dirty Rooster was just getting started. Wrecker had done his time as a prospect, just like every other member of the Washington DC chapter of the Reaper Bastards. Wrecker wasn't only my new club brother but a true brother from a different mother. We did everything together, from bangin' pussy to raising hell in our neighborhood since high school.

I'd been a patched-in member of the Reaper Bastards for only a year and was next in line someday to hold the gavel as Prez of the DC chapter. Trick was the current prez. He was also my dad and a mean motherfucker too.

Even having the sweetbutt suck me off didn't help clear the anger brewing inside me lately. Her name started with a T—Tina or Tracy?—and I took her out back behind the building. She took as much of my dick as she could into her mouth and swallowed. When I was done feeding her my load, I shoved my drained dick back in my jeans and zipped up. I took her hand, pulling her up off her knees. She was pretty, with short blonde spiked-out hair. She was a bit drunk already, her black eyeliner streaked down her cheeks with tears from choking on me.

I gave her cheek a soft smack, then shoved a thumb in between her lips. "You're such a dirty girl."

She looked at me and licked my thumb. "I can't help myself, Heavy. Your giant cock tastes so fucking good."

I smacked her on the ass and followed her through the back door and back into the Dirty Rooster. I walked up to the bar and ordered a shot of tequila. When I downed it, I slammed the glass on the bar, telling the bartender to pour me another. After the second shot, I looked down at the other end of the bar and saw a cute girl with long dark hair. She was standing behind Tye and some other girl I pegged as the cute girl's friend. Tye had been a Reaper Bastard for several years now and was really close to Trick. He liked to smack girls around. I'd once seen him drag a sweetbutt by her hair across the dirty floor of the clubhouse. He was a club brother, but that didn't mean I had to like the greasy prick.

I could tell the cute, dark-haired girl wasn't a sweetbutt right away by the clothes she wore because it wasn't the usual skimpy shit. She wore a hoodie jacket that looked two sizes too big, which only had me wondering what her tits looked like under it. The girl had that innocent vibe. She was a lamb among the pack of filthy fuckin' wolves.

My reflexes were quick the moment Tye raised his hand, ready to hit the girl when she barked at him.

"Fuck off, she's not your sweetbutt. She's *mine*," I growled, gripping his wrist and wanting to rip his throat out.

Tye jerked his arm away. "Go ahead, you can have the little cunt!"

I took the beer from the girl and set it on the bar. She yelped when I grabbed her by the waist and lifted her. She was so little and light. I hauled her easily onto my shoulder, then carried her away.

"What the fuck are you doing?! Put me down, asshole!" The girl shouted, her hands holding onto the back of my cut.

She was a brave little girl for calling me an asshole. I smacked her ass, and she squeaked, all the while wiggling as I carried her out the front door. I heard a few Bastards who stood outside, laughing. When I set the girl down on her feet, she backed away, raising her fists. Her cheeks were flushed, and she glared at me. It was sexy as fuck.

I jutted out my jaw and pointed at my chin, "Go ahead, throw one right here, darlin'." She swung, landing one on my cheek. More laughter from my Bastard brothers. "That all you got, little girl?"

The girl's bottom lip quivered.

"Just get outta here," I said, heading my way back inside.

"But I don't have anywhere to go!"

I turned back around and glared at her, gritting my teeth. "I guarantee if you go back inside, my brothers will pull a train on your virgin ass!"

"What about my friend, Krista? Will your brothers gang-rape her too?"

"If she's with Tye, then that's what'll happen."

Her eyes welled with tears then, and she began to cry, folding her arms across her chest.

I groaned, knowing this girl was gonna be trouble. I took two steps toward her. "You really don't have anywhere to go?"

She sniffled, wiping her nose with the sleeve of her hoodie. "No. I ran away from home tonight. I'm never going back. Ever."

At the age of twenty-five, I'd already fucked a shit ton of women, mostly club whores. I wasn't used to pretty girls who looked innocent and clean like this one. There was no way she could go back inside. "Did you pack a bag?"

"Yeah."

"Your parents will report you missing, and then when the cops come sniffing around, they'll track you right to my clubhouse."

"I left my backpack in Tye's van. I just need to figure out what to do next."

"Okay. I'll take you back inside." I tilted her chin. It was dark out, but I could tell her eyes were a lighter shade of brown than her dark hair. "You stay right next to me and don't *ever* leave my sight. Understand?"

"Yes, I understand."

"What's your name?"

"Danika. Danika Stevens."

"Call me Heavy."

CHAPTER 3
DANIKA

REAPER BASTARDS

MC

WASHINGTON, D.C.

Heavy was an asshole, just like Tye, but he looked good and smelled much better. But tossing me over his shoulder like I was a piece of meat infuriated me, even though he didn't threaten or try to hit me like Tye had. I decided to take my chances with Heavy and stay close to him as we went back inside the bar. Both the vodka and beer kicked in, and I stumbled a bit, bumping face first into Heavy's back.

He spun around, wrapping his arm over my shoulders, pulling me close. "You're like a tadpole, squirming around and shit. Stay right here next to me."

It was smoky and dimly lit inside, but I could see his dark eyes and the corner of his mouth lifted. Feeling his hard body close to mine was unnerving. Then a quick flash of images invaded my mind.

The feel of his rough hands on my body. The stink of the liquor and weed on his breath.

I panicked and pressed my hands against Heavy's chest, pushing away. But he held me there, his eyes fierce. "You're safe with me, Dani. I won't hurt you."

"You promise?" Asking an outlaw to promise me *anything* sounded so ridiculous.

He held up three fingers. "Scout's honor."

I smiled then, shrugging my shoulders, and moved closer.

I spotted Krista and Tye sitting with a few other people at a table. I was both annoyed and hurt that Krista felt Tye was more important than me and our friendship. When our eyes met, I arched a brow and flipped her the bird.

I walked with Heavy to the bar, and he handed me a beer. Another Reaper Bastard approached us, with both his arms draped over two women barely dressed in bikini tops and short skirts. He staggered and weaved, and his eyes were bloodshot and glassy.

He bumped his fist with Heavy's. "I'm so shit-faced, brother, I can't even remember my fuckin' name!"

They both hooted and howled like two savage wolves.

Heavy introduced me to him. "Danika, this is my club brother, Wrecker. He's the reason the Reaper Bastards are here tonight. We're celebrating his patchin'-in."

Wrecker leaned forward, grinning as the two girls giggled. "Hey, Dan... Danika."

Even though Heavy hardly talked to me at all that night, his hearty laugh made him seem more likable, and I felt a little more at ease around him.

It was two a.m. when the bar closed, and the Reaper Bastards were moving the party to their clubhouse. I ignored Krista all night but watched as she left with Tye and a few other club members. She didn't look my way as she walked out. My heart sank, and I felt abandoned by the only friend I thought I had. But if she was riding with Tye to the clubhouse, I worried that something terrible would happen to her.

I looked at Heavy. "I can't just let her go to your clubhouse by herself, and I left my backpack in Tye's van. Will you take me there?"

Heavy's eyes followed Tye, and the other Reaper Bastards exit the bar. He nodded his head to the big man leading them out. "That big man in front of them is Trick. He's the club's president. Stay away from him, cause if he wants to claim you, he can, and there's nothing I can do about it. Understood?"

"Yes, Heavy."

He took my hand and led me out of the bar. "You ever rode on a bike?"

"Uh. No, but I'm a quick learner."

We walked over to the parked motorcycles and stopped in front of his. It was a black Harley with real high handlebars and hard saddlebags.

"You need a lid," Heavy said, then walked over to another club member who pulled out a helmet from his saddlebag. He came back and placed it on my head. He snapped the straps together under my chin and handed me a pair of sunglasses.

"I get on the bike first. You climb on behind me and put your feet on those footboards. Then just hang on to me. Got it?"

"Got it."

Climbing on behind Heavy was easy, and I wrapped my arms around his waist. He started the bike, and the pipes rumbled low and loud. We pulled out in a tight group, and Trick was in the front leading his club, while Heavy rode last and in the back. I held onto him, my hands touching his leather cut, the wind pushing against us. The vibration and thundering roar of all the motorcycles was thrilling, especially to a girl like me who'd never been on one before, let alone sit behind an outlaw biker.

The pack stopped at a red light in the heart of the city. Heavy planted his feet and turned his head toward me. "I can't even feel you back there. You're so little, like a tadpole."

That was the second time Heavy called me that. I was going to say something nasty but then decided not to since it was better than being called a cunt.

When the light turned green, and the group revved their throttles, Heavy left the pack and turned an immediate right onto a one-way street.

I tapped him on the shoulder. "Where are we going?!"

"Not to the clubhouse!" he barked back as he pulled in the clutch, switching gears.

I became frightened then, wondering if he was some deranged lunatic who was going to take me down a dead-end street and rape or kill me. I would be the perfect victim since he knew I was a runaway, and my parents didn't even give a shit. For a moment, I thought of jumping off. I looked down as the bike sped up, and the ground was just a blur. Quick images of broken bones and blood flashed through my mind.

"Stop the bike! Please!" I shouted, leaning away from him.

He reached back, placing his hand on the back of my calf, "Relax, Dani. I'm taking you somewhere else. It'll be safer."

I exhaled a sigh of relief and leaned forward, wrapping my arms around Heavy again as he rode us out of the inner city of DC and onto the highway.

CHAPTER 4
HEAVY

REAPER BASTARDS

MC

WASHINGTON, D.C.

What the fuck was I doing with a teenage runaway on the back of my bike? My club didn't need the law on our fucking backs and sniffing around the clubhouse for two goddamn teenage girls. Danika had *trouble* written all over her, and it would land on the club and me. And then she started to cry when I carried her out of the bar. I fucking *hated* to see a chick cry. I only liked to see a chick cry when I choked and fucked her or when she was gagging on my hard dick.

Tye was a fuck up. He never followed club laws, and he did whatever the fuck he wanted to benefit Tye. Bringing the girls to a patch-in party was way beyond stupid. I kept my anger in check all night even though I wanted to smash my fist into his face. Trick didn't seem to have a problem with it. Since he was the Prez, I just kept my mouth shut and my eyes on Danika.

Danika held onto me tight as I rode out of the city and checked into the Spotlight Motel, a popular spot for truckers off the main interstate. When she followed me into the motel room, I shoved the key into my pocket. "Lock the door when I leave and do not open it for anyone. I'll come back in before dawn."

I turned to go, but she grabbed my arm. "Wait! What about Krista? If you didn't take me to the clubhouse, then she *must* be in danger."

"Nothing I can do about that."

She let go of my arm and sat on the bed. Her head dropped and shut her eyes. "I left my backpack in Tye's van. It's all I have. We should never have gone to your club's party. If something bad happens to Krista, I'll never be able to forgive myself."

I'd known of young girls like her that ran from a bad life at home. They were the ones who ended up as the property of a diamond club like mine. Then they were pimped out, strung out on drugs, and sometimes ended up dead.

Danika was a pretty girl, and she was gutsy for taking a swing at my face earlier that night. I was starting to like her, and I never liked anyone.

I walked over to the bed and tilted her chin. There was better light in the room, and I could see her eyes better. A lighter shade than her dark hair. *Hazel.* "It's not your fault. I'll go by the clubhouse and check on her and get your backpack."

Her brows shot up. "Would you do that?"

"Yeah."

She was off the bed and threw her arms around my neck. "Thank you, Heavy."

I breathed in Danika's fresh scent and couldn't stop myself from pulling her small body closer. My hand twisted into her dark hair and pulled. Her lips parted, craving to be kissed. I smashed mine over hers for a little taste.

She moaned, and my dick started to get hard.

I released her. "Then I'm gettin' you on the first bus out of here in the morning."

I walked out of the room, slamming the door hard. Danika Stevens was too young and too clean to be around a dangerous asshole like me. I'd do some hardcore damage to that girl, and I had to get rid of her quick.

I twisted the throttle wide open back onto the interstate. I rode to the clubhouse in DC, a large warehouse in the southeast district, beside the Potomac River. I spotted Tye's van parked out in the gravel lot as I rode in through the bay doors and parked my bike beside the others. My club brother, Rufus, was shit-faced, pulling his bike up the cement ramp and into the burn-out pit. Brothers were shouting and whistling as Rufus placed the front tire up against a cement wall. Standing the bike up, he revved the throttle, and the back tire spun. Half the clubhouse was covered in a plume of white smoke, as the bike's pipes roared, and club whores waved their hands at the smoke, coughing and laughing.

I climbed off the bike, and I scanned the clubhouse looking for Tye and the girl, Krista. I didn't see them at the bar, then looked over at the pool tables to see Wrecker laying on one, passed the fuck out. I saw Trick standing by the bar with a chick who looked too young to even be legal. His eyes met mine, and he waved me over.

"Where's Tye?" I asked when I approached.

"He's havin' a little fun with that young squeeze of his."

I clenched my jaw as my father's bloodshot eyes darted to look behind me. "Where's the other one? Thought she was with you?"

"The little bitch was a fuckin lightweight, almost puked all over me and the bike. I ditched her on the way here. Left her at a metro bus stop."

My brothers, who stood around us, laughed, but Trick looked pissed. When he downed a shot of his favorite whiskey, he stepped up and stood only inches from my face. We were the same height and build. There was no doubt we were father and son. I hated him, and he knew it.

He glared at me with bloodshot eyes. "I had plans for that girl."

I stood my ground. "What plans?"

The brothers standing around, stopped laughing.

"You and me. Outside," Trick growled.

I followed him out big bay doors toward the graveled parking lot where Tye's van was parked. I had a good guess that Tye was in it with the girl, but it was eerily quiet—no laughter, no screams.

Trick stopped short, only a few yards away from the van and lit a joint. He didn't pass it to me since he liked his dope and didn't share it. "You're not holding the gavel anytime soon, son. Better reign in some of that hate you have for me. Don't show it around our brothers. It makes them uneasy, and before you know it, they start questioning their loyalty to the Reaper Bastards."

I wanted to bash my knuckles into his face. He never had one fucking loyal bone in his ruthless body. It was all about what was in it for him, not the club.

I was done with this father to son talk. "What's this plan?"

Trick took another hit off his joint, holding it in then exhaled before he told me. "Tye wanted to push those girls into whoring and to help push the meth. He's a stupid son of a bitch. Those girls are worth a lot more. I put them up for auction and sold them to the highest bidder."

"Who?"

"Some suits. They're Russian. Fifty grand apiece. Those slant-eyed Yakuza motherfuckers came in second."

"The Bastards don't deal with those white-collar pieces of shit. Wasn't it you who always told us we'd never do business with them?"

I turned and walked away with even more hate than I thought I could have for my own father. Krista's fate was sealed, and there was nothing I could do about it. But I had to get Danika on the first bus and miles away from DC.

"Don't turn your back on me, Hendrix! I'll take your patch and slice the Bastard ink right off your fuckin skin!" Trick threatened, and I believed him too.

I halted my steps. "There wasn't a club vote on this deal you made with the Russians, but you're the president of this club. What you say, the Bastards make happen. I'm going back inside to get my dick wet."

CHAPTER 5
DANIKA

REAPER BASTARDS

MC

WASHINGTON, D.C.

Heavy slammed the motel door so hard, it shook the walls, and a framed picture fell to the floor. I sat back down on the bed and touched my lips which still tingled. I was terrified at first when Heavy pulled my hair, his eyes full of hungry lust that I'd seen in another man's eyes. But when he kissed me, it sent all my senses reeling. His tongue was ruthless and demanding. I moaned, and he let me go like I was a hot flame that burned him.

I lay on the bed, hugged my knees to my chest, and began to cry. I was alone and afraid. No one ever protected me—not even my own mother. She hated me and even when Jack began to touch me. I always felt it was my fault, especially when my mother looked at me with disgust, and maybe even with jealousy. Krista was the only one I thought was my friend, but after what happened at the bar, I felt like she stabbed me in the back.

The only person who showed me any bit of kindness was a dangerous outlaw biker. I didn't think things through when I packed my bag and ran away earlier that night. I only had five hundred bucks, and I knew that wouldn't get me far. Heavy said he would get me on a bus in the morning. The reality of feeling even more alone and not knowing what would happen spiraled me down into depression. I was living and breathing fear.

I must have cried myself to sleep when I felt the bed creak and shift. I woke up to see Heavy leaning over me.

"Wake up, Danika," he said, his voice deep and gruff.

I rolled over and climbed out of bed. I stood, rubbed my eyes, and yawned. "Is Krista okay?"

"No. She's dead."

"What?"

He held out my backpack. "If I don't get you on a bus now, Dani, you'll be just as dead as she is!"

I broke down sobbing, and my body began to tremble. "But she can't be dead."

Heavy's solid arms came around me. I dug my fingers into the front of his vest. "It's a fucked-up shitshow. Tye had Krista in his van; she OD'd on some bad shit he gave her. My prez had plans to sell you both to some Russians for a good ton of cash. They won't be too happy when their merchandise is dead, and the other one got away."

"I'm scared."

"I know you are." He leaned away, gripping my arms. "But we're wasting time. Get your shoes on, and let's get the fuck outta here."

I clung tightly to Heavy while we rode his bike to the Greyhound bus station as the sun was coming up. I bought a one-way ticket to Atlantic City, New Jersey. As people stood in line to board the bus, I sniffled, my eyes swollen from crying on the ride there. Heavy shoved his hand down his jeans pocket.

He took my hand and placed a rolled-up wad of cash in it. "It's only a grand, but that's all I got on me. When you get to Atlantic City, find a woman's shelter. You should be safer there than sleeping on the streets. Find a job flipping burgers, pumping gas—anything—'cause the money will run out quick."

I looked down at the wad of cash in my hand. I'd never seen a thousand dollars before and wondered what kinds of bad and unlawful things Heavy did to get it. He was dangerous, and so were the other men in his club.

"Why?" I whispered.

"Why what?"

"Why are you helping me?"

I looked up at his eyes. They were a dark, cold gray. "Not sure why. You're gutsy, and I like that. You must be running away from something or someone at home. You got dealt a bad card last night, was in the wrong place at the wrong time. Pretty girls like you are just prey to bad men like me. I figured you need a second chance."

Just then, I saw the man standing before me. Seeing through the mean exterior of tattoos and leather, Heavy was good-looking, and I suddenly felt a flutter in my stomach.

I threw my arms around his neck. "Thank you. I'll pay you back the money."

His warm hands pressed against my back. "You don't owe me anything, and once you get on that bus, you're never goin' to see me again."

I was the last one to step on the bus. When I sat in a seat beside the window, I began to cry again as I watched Heavy swing a leg over his bike and ride away. He saved my life. I hoped someday I'd be able to pay him back.

PART 2
7 YEARS LATER

CHAPTER 6
HEAVY

REAPER BASTARDS

MC

WASHINGTON, D.C.

Trick's business venture with the Russian mob backfired on him once they learned of Krista's death and the disappearance of Danika. Tye took care of burying Krista somewhere in the dense woods surrounding the National Zoo in DC. She was reported missing, and her picture with a description was all over the local news. Tye had a rap sheet of too many fuck-ups, so the club stripped him of his patches. Since he was a Reaper Bastard for five years, the club voted him out instead of dragging him out somewhere to dig his own grave. I only told Wrecker how I'd put Danika on a bus, but he barely remembered that night altogether.

Things didn't get any better for Trick either because the club lost all respect for him. A year later, I called all the patched-in members for church at the clubhouse. Every club member voted me in as the prez of the DC Chapter, and I stripped Trick of his patch. He was left as the lowest-ranking member but could vote and attend church. Wrecker was my brother from another mother, so it was only natural he was made my VP. And, there was Roadkill. He'd only been patched in for about a year, but he proved himself time and time again when things got messy. Roadkill was deranged, and the things I saw him do to men were downright medieval, especially with his use of sharp knives and surgical instruments. He didn't say much, but his eyes lit up when bloody violence was going to happen. I made Roadkill the sergeant at arms.

The Reaper Bastards made a ton of money selling pussy. The Washington DC Chapter ran the strip clubs in the city and used our club whores to sell the pussy and drugs. Wealthy businessmen and politicians just handed over tons of cash, and the club had three-figure earnings in the bank. The pussy business was just as profitable as the drugs and sometimes made us a bit more. Our whores helped hustle the drugs and pussy. The only drawback to our whores hustling was the liability; some used and became worthless methheads rather than bringing in the profit.

There's a saying that goes something like *use the gifts that God gave you.* It was either God or Satan, but one of them gave me the gift that women loved—a monster dick. I used it well and fucked a ton of pussy since the age of fifteen. My real name is Hendrix Stone, but everyone called me Heavy since I was, well, hung like a raging bull. When I patched in as a Reaper Bastard, the chicks flocked like groupies at a rock concert. They hoped for a chance to see my heavy dick. Some wanted to suck or fuck it just to gain bragging rights. I got a good video camera to film some of my own amateur porn with women who were willing, and they loved it. I uploaded some of my homemade videos to porn sites, which brought on big ideas in my head. I wanted to make more and more fuckin' money since you could never have enough of that...well, along with tight pussy.

I wanted my club to get into the porn business and reap the rewards with the big sharks in the porn industry. I brought this new business venture up for a vote during church at the clubhouse and all members were in. I set up a big party at the Pink Pussy Dollhouse, a strip club we owned, for strippers and club whores who wanted to be part of what we called DC's Dirty Dolls. The club was packed with half-naked strippers dancing on poles and my Reaper Bastard brothers, but I noticed Trick didn't show up. That was fine with me since I hated to be within eye-sight of him anyway. Loud stripper music blared through the speakers, while the three bartenders were pouring drinks and taking the high-dollar tips.

I sat beside Wrecker in a booth decked out in leopard print. He rolled a nice fat joint and passed it to me. I took a hit while I drank a beer and caught a good buzz.

I passed the joint back to Wrecker when he jumped, looking down under the table. "Teeth! Watch the teeth, darlin'."

I looked down and chuckled.

A blonde chick with big fake tits and braces was under the table, sucking his dick. She looked up with big doe eyes and pouted. "Whoops! Sorry, I just got the braces last week."

Wrecker smiled down at her, shoving a thumb in her mouth. "You're gonna need plenty of practice with those new braces, but not on me, darlin'. Go on, get outta here."

The girl crawled out from under the table and I laughed when Wrecker smacked her on the ass as she walked away.

Wrecker was zipping himself up when I caught sight of a dark-haired girl walking up the steps to the center stage. It was the girl—Danika. There were times I'd imagined what her body looked like underneath those baggy clothes she wore seven years ago. There's nothing left to imagine now, 'cause she was dressed in a fishnet catsuit, with black, high-heeled boots, and nothing else. Her tits were real and gorgeous as fuck, and there was no little patch of hair...that pussy was bald.

I nudged Wrecker when Danika began to dance. "Remember that young chick at your patch-in party years ago? The one I put on a bus?"

"Yeah?" Wrecker said.

"That's the same little bitch on the fucking stage right now."

Wrecker's red glazed-over eyes steered to the stage.

"*Hot Damn!*" Wrecker hollered.

That's when I shot out of the booth and marched toward the stage.

I stormed up the steps to the stage before Danika could hook her leg around the pole. She gasped, and her eyes went wide the moment she recognized me. "Heavy?"

I clenched my jaw, and she yelped when I lifted her onto my shoulder. She was just as tiny as she was seven years ago. I carried her down the steps and walked into a VIP room, hearing the hoots and hollers behind me.

I slammed the door and set her down. She flipped her long dark hair, her eyes all fierce and sexy when she glared at me.

I moved toward her.

She stepped back.

My hand shot out, wrapping around her throat. "What the fuck are you doing here?"

Her soft hands grabbed at my tight grip. "Making a shit ton of money; that's what I'm doing here! Let me go!"

I let her go and breathed in deep. I was so full of rage, that I felt blood boiling in my veins.

CHAPTER 7
DANI

REAPER BASTARDS

MC

WASHINGTON, D.C.

Heavy looked the same as he did seven years ago, but even deadlier with those cold, steel eyes. When he let me go, he stepped back, clenching his fists, his nostrils flared.

But he was quick, and in the next breath, he reached out, spinning me around. I faced the wall and slapped my hands on it.

"Wait!" I cried out.

"Shut up." He grunted. I heard him unzipping his jeans. "Spread your legs."

I took a wide step and arched my back, my heeled boots hiking my ass up even higher. I turned my head to watch him out of the corner of my eye, breathing fast.

Heavy reached down and roughly ripped a hole in the fishnet between my thighs. He spit in his palm and reached down. I wondered for so many years what his dick looked like, felt like, then suddenly he pressed the tip right at my eager opening.

When he took hold of my hips, I held my breath, waiting for Heavy to slam all of himself into me, but instead, he was nice and slow. His dick was unbelievably thick, and I cried out, but pushed back, needing all of him.

"You're so damn tight," he groaned next to my shoulder as he drove the rest of that monster deep, stretching and filling me up.

My head fell back, relishing the feel of him as he pulled out and drove back in again.

Someone pounded on the door.

"Goddamnit!" Heavy fumed, pulling out. "What the fuck!"

I turned from the wall, raking both my hands through my hair, trying to catch my breath as Heavy zipped up and moved to the door.

He opened it, and a big bearded man wearing a Reaper Bastard cut shoved Bobby inside.

Bobby stumbled back, holding his hands up to ward off the biker. "Hey, man! I don't want any trouble, just wanted to check on my girl!"

"Your girl?" Heavy asked, glaring at me.

Bobby held my bag over his shoulder and smiled when he saw me. "There you are, Dani! Are you okay?"

"The stupid shit followed you back here, Prez. Started pounding on the door," the big biker grumbled.

Heavy slapped him on the shoulder. "Thanks, Roadkill. I got this."

The biker turned and left the room.

He called that biker Roadkill?

Heavy turned his attention back to Bobby. "Who the fuck are you?"

Bobby shrugged his shoulders, straightening out his suit jacket. "I'm Big Bobby Decker." He pulled out a business card and offered it to Heavy.

He snatched my purse from Bobby, then slapped the card out of his hand. "Another white-collar motherfucker who thinks he's mobbed up."

"I'm Dani Storm's manager! She works for me!" Bobby was pompous enough to open his mouth and get a fist smashed into it. I knew because I'd seen it happen before.

Heavy dropped my bag on the couch and twisted his fists into the lapels of Bobby's jacket, baring his teeth. "She doesn't work for you anymore, pissant. She works for the Reaper Bastards." He turned Bobby around, shoving him toward the door. "Now, get the fuck out of my club."

Bobby looked at me with a nervous smile before he left the room. "I'll sort this all out with these guys tomorrow, baby."

Heavy chuckled then. "He's not your manager. He's just your suitcase pimp, and he looks old enough to be your damn granddad!"

I folded my arms over my chest, suddenly feeling naked and vulnerable in front of him. I lifted my chin. "You didn't have to do that to Bobby. He's done so much for me. He keeps me fed, sets me up so I can live at his place, and buys me nice clothes. He gives me everything I need and treats me with things I want!"

"Yeah, that's what pimps do, Dani. I'm bettin' he's fucked all your holes to keep you just where he wants you, making *him* good money with that pussy of yours."

Like a broken dam, I felt the tears roll down my cheeks, and I began to sob. I was both exhilarated and exhausted with anxiety when I saw the dangerous man who saved my life seven long years ago.

I balled my fists and drew back to hit him, but he blocked me. "You swung at me before, bitch. But never again."

I jerked my arm from his grasp. "You know nothing about me, you arrogant heartless asshole! I told Bobby it was a bad idea to come here tonight."

I moved toward the door, but Heavy snatched me around the waist.

"Let me go!" I shouted, struggling against him, but there was no use. He was much stronger.

He spun me around, pressing me tightly against him, and pinned my arms behind me. "Didn't you hear me? You're Reaper Bastard property now."

I was breathing too fast after feeling the leather of his cut brush against my nipples which were hard since he carried me into the room.

"You don't own me! No one fucking owns me!" I shot back.

His brows were furrowed, his glare penetrating. "You've come to the wrong place at the wrong time, Dani...just like seven years ago. You should never have come back. You're staying for good this time and making my club a shit ton of money."

Heavy released me, grabbed my bag off the couch, and tossed it at me. "You're not showing off the merchandise here tonight. Put some fuckin' clothes on."

CHAPTER 8
DANI

REAPER BASTARDS

MC

WASHINGTON, D.C.

I'd never let some chick get under my skin, but Danika sure as hell did when she got up on that stage at the Dollhouse showing off her tits and ass to everyone. I was so fuckin' pissed that all I wanted to do was inflict some pain to punish the little bitch. I enjoyed shoving my dick up inside that tight pussy of hers in the VIP before she could bat those pretty brown eyes at me. When the party ended, Danika dressed in actual clothes, climbed on the back of my bike and ended up at my house right outside DC city limits.

I parked the bike in the garage, and Danika followed me into the house, clutching her bag to her chest.

"The house is nothing extravagant, but it's clean," I said as I led her past the living room and down the hall. I showed her the spare room and turned on the light. There was no bed, only a mattress and box spring on the floor with sheets, blankets, and a pillow. "You can sleep in here."

Danika entered the room, and I turned to leave.

"Wait!" she called out.

"What now?"

She was walking a very thin line with me that night. I didn't want to see her cry or bitch and moan about the mattress or any other fucking thing.

"I have money. I can stay at a hotel tomorrow if you take me to one."

I leaned against the doorframe and stared at her for a moment. Those light brown eyes of hers were giving me a semi-hard-on. "My club is at war with the Bloody Aces. The clubhouse isn't safe, especially for you. Hotels are out of the question."

She turned to look at the mattress, then back at me. "You're not going to rape me again, are you?"

Oh, she was trying to pick a fight.

"Well, you didn't say *no.*" I scratched my beard. "And I do recall seeing your hands pressed on the wall, just waitin' for my dick to slide up in you."

"You asshole!" she shouted, throwing her bag at me.

I caught it and tossed it on the floor next to her feet. "The bathroom is down the hall. Get some sleep."

I would've made Danika sleep in my bed with me, but I slept alone—*always*. If I fucked a chick in my bed, they were never allowed to sleep in it with me afterward.

A few days later, Danika wanted to call her ex-pimp, Bobby, in Atlantic City. She told me he must be worried sick about her and that she wanted to get some of her clothes. I shot that down quickly and gave her some cash and sent her out shopping with Lacey Lust—the blonde with the new braces who sucked on Wrecker's dick at the party. I sent one of our new prospects to watch over the girls all day while they shopped at the mall since we were at war with the Bloody Aces MC. They took three of our girls a year ago and sold two of them to a sinister cartel family south across the border into Mexico. Roadkill and two other brothers went down and got the girls back, but they were cut up and severely beaten, messing them up in the head forever. The third girl was pretty but didn't make it back alive. The Bloody Aces killed her in a snuff film.

We had another run-in with the Bloody Aces only a month ago. Nolan Reynolds was one of those white-collar mobbed-up types who ran the MGM Casino in Maryland with politicians and rich tycoons lining his pockets. He paid us Reaper Bastards a hundred grand to find any leads on a missing girl. We found out the Bloody Aces were in bed with this Caruso crime family in Atlantic City and killed that missing girl in another snuff film. When they kidnapped Nolan's wife, Gina, he needed our help to get her back alive. We found her in some shitty motel in Virginia with Jimmy Caruso. One of the members of the Bloody Aces MC they called Maggot cut Gina's face up badly, so Nolan put a bullet in his head. We took Maggot's bike, stripping it and selling off the parts while Roadkill axed off Maggot's head and hands, then had them delivered to the Bloody Aces clubhouse. It was a clear message that their club and their bloody business in snuff films was over.

While Danika was out shopping, I sat at the bar in the Pink Pussy Dollhouse, waiting for Wrecker and Roadkill to show up. I pulled out my phone and made a call to Nolan Reynolds. He'd be the one to set us up with the perfect place to shoot our first film.

"The director, the girls, and a few of us Reaper Bastards are going to use one of those fancy suites you got there at the MGM this weekend. We're shooting some scenes for our porn film."

"For fuck's sake," Nolan grumbled over the phone.

I chuckled. "Just for two days. We'll use that one called the Presidential Suite. Looks like it's got some good lighting from what I could tell from pics on the internet."

Silence over the phone.

"Damnit. Okay. The suite is yours for the weekend. Just leave everything the way you found it."

I lit a joint and clicked on the link to the site that Dani texted me earlier that day. It was called "Big Bobby's Bodacious Babes," showing other girls along with Danika, staring as *Dani Storm*. I clicked on the image of a naked Dani, wrapping her arms across her tits with a sexy pout to her full lips.

I watched as the video streamed Dani lying on a lounge beside a pool on a sunny day. Two men enter the scene, and after getting her out of a black bikini, Dani worked their hard dicks. She sat on her knees while jacking them both with her hands and sucked on one, then the other. I saw the look of innocence in her eyes that I remembered from seven years ago. When the DP scene started, and they began to fuck her pussy and ass, my dick was getting hard under the bar. I shifted in my stool and then tipped back a shot of whiskey. Having a full hard-on with the kind of dick I carried gets all jacked up in a pair of jeans.

"Hot damn! Is that your chick, Danika?" Wrecker asked as he slapped a hand on my shoulder while peering over my shoulder to look at my phone.

"She's not my chick. Dani is just property like all our other club whores, and she'll bring in some big money." I closed down the site and took another hit off the joint.

Wrecker planted himself on the stool next to me as the bartender slid a beer to him. "Well, it sure did *look* like she was your chick when you carried her bare-ass-up on your shoulder the other night. She's living at your place now, too, ain't she?"

"Stop bustin' my fuckin balls, Wrecker."

When Roadkill walked in, they both followed me down the hall into one of the VIP rooms. We sat on the couches, and I passed what was left of my joint to Roadkill.

"We've hired a good film director named Stanley Kane", Wrecker said. "He's flying in from LA this weekend. The three girls chosen as DC's Dirty Dolls will be Dani Storm, Roxi Wylde, and Busty Braces."

Roadkill held in a hit too long and coughed it out.

I just shook my head at Wrecker. "If that's what you're calling her, okay, but she's Lacey Lust, dumbass. I just got off the phone with Nolan Reynolds before you two got here. We have the best suite at the MGM for two days to shoot some scenes."

"Who's the lucky guy that gets to fuck them girls?" Roadkill asked.

"That'll be our brother, Hammer."

One night while partying at the clubhouse, I was shitfaced and told Hammer to whip out his dick so we could measure ours side by side. Hammer fucked anything that sat still long enough and sported a woody when he found the club was getting into the porn business. When I approached him about being the star of the film with the Dirty Dolls, he probably shot a load all over himself.

CHAPTER 9
DANI

REAPER BASTARDS

MC

WASHINGTON, D.C.

Heavy handed me a load of cash to go shopping with, and Lacey picked me up from his house. I didn't pack much in the bag I brought from Atlantic City and resorted to just wearing a pair of cut-off jean shorts, a black tank, and my black-heeled boots. She drove us to the mall while Eddy, one of Heavy's prospects, followed us on his bike. He was all inked up and big as a bear, but with his boyish face, he looked more like a teddy bear than a grizzly. Lacey was a dancer at the Dollhouse with pretty blonde hair, curvy hips, and a nice set of fake tits. She seemed to hold back and gave me closed-lip smiles because I think she was a little embarrassed by her new set of braces. It was just nice to get away from Heavy and his grumpy stares the past few days. I enjoyed Lacey's company as we shopped at a mall, trying on both cute and sexy outfits together. We giggled when we made Eddy carry our shopping bags. He was pretty pissed by the time we left the mall, but he did exactly as Heavy told him to do—keep a protective watch over both Lacey and me.

"Thank you for taking me out shopping today," I said to Lacey as she drove us to the Dollhouse to meet up with Heavy.

"You're so welcome, honey. I love to shop, plus I'd do anything to help Wrecker and the Reaper Bastards."

I saw her blue eyes light up and her cheeks flush when she mentioned Wrecker. "Aww, you like him, don't you? Your eyes lit up! He's a total hottie; I don't blame you."

"Yeah, I do. Very much. Every time he looks at me, I get tingles in the rights spots! We've never fucked, but I've given him three blow jobs. But he looks at me like he does all the girls at the Dollhouse. The third time I sucked him was at the Reaper Bastards Video party. But I didn't do so great with these new braces. He told me to go practice sucking on someone else's dick..." Lacey stopped smiling, and her sad eyes turned back to the road as she drove.

Wrecker was an asshole. "Then turn the tables on him, Lacey."

"I *was* under a table when I gave him the blow job."

"What I mean is show him you're not the least bit interested in him anymore. If he's at the Dollhouse, pay extra attention to a customer who wants to watch you dance. I'll bet he notices then and maybe even gets a little jealous."

She let out a high-pitched giggle. "Wrecker and the Reaper Bastards don't get jealous. I mean, yeah, some have old ladies that wear their property patches, and those girls are golden. They're not to be touched, and they're protected by every member of the club. The rest of us girls are just sweetbutts, and a Reaper Bastard can take his pick, depending on his mood."

"That's just so barbaric and unfair. What if I wanted to hit on one of the Reaper Bastards? The single ones, I mean. Can I have my choice of who I want between *my* legs?"

Lacey looked at me again, but this time her smiling eyes were serious. "It's a man's world when it comes to an Outlaw MC, Dani. I learned that a long time ago. Some of us girls are lucky and become an old lady to a good man in the club, but some don't. Those who don't are passed around and used up. There's a saying for that in this world: *Rode hard and put away wet.* I don't want to be one of those deadbeat bitches, strung out on drugs. I want to be someone's old lady. I want to be Wrecker's old lady."

"Most men I've known are just like that; some are far worse. I learned when I was young, what men wanted. They want power. They want control. Those real sadistic motherfuckers will beat you and use you up until they're bored and done with you. Then they toss you away like trash or pass you onto someone else just as cruel. So, to stay alive and halfway sane, I evened up the score. I learned what to say, how to dress, how to dance, and even how to fuck. It was all about survival."

As Lacey pulled into the parking lot of the Dollhouse, we saw Heavy's bike parked alongside the others. We entered the club, and Eddy led us down the hall to the VIP room—the same room that Heavy carried me into that night at the party. I remember the feel of his huge dick as he slid inside me, and my stomach fluttered.

Eddy knocked three times and then opened the door. "The girls are back, Prez."

I followed Lacey into the smoke-filled room that smelled of weed to see Heavy sitting on one couch and Wrecker and Roadkill sitting on a couch opposite him.

Heavy slouched lazily, wearing a black wifebeater, jeans, and black boots. He looked so damn sexy and cocky at once.

"You did good, Prospect. Now go out and watch the bikes until we're set to ride over to the clubhouse."

Lacey plopped down on the couch next to Wrecker when Heavy pointed to the space beside him. "Sit here, Dani."

I walked over and planted my ass up close to him so that our thighs touched. The side of his lip lifted in a half-smile. "When we get home tonight, I want you to try on all the clothes you bought with my money."

"As long as you don't rip any holes in them," I bit back.

Heavy leaned his head back and laughed, surprising me to see him in a lighter mood than usual.

Roadkill passed a joint to him. "You paid for those clothes with *my* money, so I can do whatever the fuck I want to them." He took a hit and held it in for a long moment and exhaled. He offered it to me. "Take a hit. Relax a bit." I leaned in as Heavy held the joint between his thumb and finger and took a hit of the sweet-tasting weed. He passed it across to Wrecker. "I checked out the link you sent. I'm impressed. You learned a lot in those seven years. Get ready for a workout on that mouth, pussy, and ass this weekend. We're set to shoot our first film in a private suite at the MGM. The director is flying in from LA; his name is Stanley Kane. You, Lacey, and Roxi are the trio as the DC's Dirty Dolls. Hammer is the male lead. He packs a good-sized dick too. We're throwing a party tonight at the clubhouse."

I held in the hit, then exhaled, feeling the high coming on. "I thought you'd be the male lead. What are you going to do? Watch while we shoot the film?"

"Of course, I am. So are Wrecker and Roadkill. You ask too many questions."

He saw me only as a commodity for the Reaper Bastards—their property. When he looked at me, all he saw was dollar signs. My fate was sealed, according to Heavy. I was just pussy, making his club filthy rich bastards.

Even the slight buzz I got off the joint couldn't calm the anger that was boiling like hot lava inside me.

"Get your fuckin' ass back here, bitch!" Heavy roared when I left the couch and stormed out of the VIP room.

I didn't have a clue where I was going, but I hated Heavy and wanted to scratch his fucking eyes out. I was so stupid to even think he would've been glad to see me after all these years. I guess I just had hope. Vain hopes and wishes of a naïve girl. He couldn't care less if I fucked every member of his club, including the prospects.

I knew I wouldn't get far, but I almost made it to the front door of the club when Heavy grabbed my arm. He spun me around, and I collided into his leather cut. I flinched when I saw the anger in his eyes and thought he was going to hit me in the face.

He bared his teeth, his jaw set. "Do not *ever* disrespect me like that again, Danika."

I pushed against his chest. "What if I do? Are you going to beat me? Rape me? Been there, done that plenty of fucking times! I'm surprised I still breathe!"

He gave me the death stare for a few moments, then released me. "You're just property—a fresh, tight hole to fuck. Nothing else."

I jumped when Heavy turned, slamming his fist into the tiled mirrors on the wall. Sharp pieces of mirror shattered, cutting into his knuckles. His blood was smeared on the broken mirror as he turned and left me, walking back down the hall into the VIP room.

I couldn't wait to see Heavy's reaction when this film director Stanley began shooting the film, and I worked on this guy,

Hammer's dick. I was going to put on a good show and see the jealousy in Heavy's furious gray eyes.

CHAPTER 10
HEAVY

REAPER BASTARDS

 **MC**

WASHINGTON, D.C.

I almost busted up Dani's pretty face in a split second but smashed my fist into the mirror instead. I walked away from her and didn't give a fuck if she walked out of the club. I ran some cold water from the bathroom sink over my cut knuckles, and it felt good, helping to calm my temper down a bit. When I was growing up, I'd seen Trick's fists bust up my mom's face so many times I lost count. Then, one day, she just up and left. I barely even remember what she looked like, and I didn't have any pictures of her.

Dani not only came back to DC, but she also came right back into Reaper Bastards territory. I planned on doing everything I could to make her regret it.

I lost the buzz off Wrecker's good weed, and for the rest of that day, all I wanted to do was fight and fuck. My brothers, along with the prospect, left the Dollhouse and rode to the clubhouse for the party. Lacey drove Dani and pulled into the lot a few minutes later as we rode in through the bay doors to park our bikes and climbed off.

The sun was just setting, and the clubhouse was full of Reaper Bastard brothers, their old ladies, a few hang-arounds, and sweetbutts. Dani steered clear of me, staying close to Lacey and Roxi. But she knew I watched every move she would make. I was playing a round of pool with my brother Bagger when Hammer arrived, riding into the clubhouse on his bike. He melted some rubber off his back tire in the burn-out pit, filling the clubhouse with clouds of smoke. Shots were passed around, and the Reaper Bastards passed Hammer around for bro hugs.

"I'm honored, brother. I'm gonna make you fuckin' proud," Hammer said as we hugged and slapped each other on the back.

Dani, Lacey, and Roxi approached arm in arm, and I introduced them to Hammer as the DC's Dirty Dolls. He looked like a Vin Diesel clone and smiled a lot, so the girls seemed to like him. A few more rounds of shots were passed out while joints were lit as we got the party started. When someone threw songs on the jukebox, Roxi set Hammer down on one of the dusty old couches to give him a lap dance.

A sweetbutt we all called Bambi came over to stand in front of me. She bent over and twerked her big ass up against my crotch. I looked over at Dani as she stood beside Lacey and a few others watching Roxi's lap dance. She glared at Bambi, her pretty lips set in a straight line.

I smiled, my eyes steering down to Bambi's fat ass in a skimpy skirt and smacked it.

Bambi giggled, flipping her jet-black hair. I spun her around, pressing her up against me. "That bodacious ass is gonna get you in a whole lot of trouble tonight, darlin'."

"I sure do hope it does," she said, as she snaked her hand down the front of my jeans.

I looked back at Dani when she rolled her eyes and turned her back. I got the reaction I was aiming for out of her and planned on getting balls deep in Bambi before the night was over. Bambi wrapped her arms around my neck and started licking my neck with her tongue. I grunted, squeezing her ass when she sucked, leaving a silver-dollar-sized hickey on my neck.

A few more bikes rolled into the clubhouse. One of them was Trick, with a girl on the back. He had the fucking balls to show up when he didn't come to the Dollhouse party.

Trick approached me with his big arm draped over the small girl he rode in with. She looked way too young to be legal, wearing barely anything that showed off a boyish figure and not the curves of a grown woman. She staggered and swayed, and she would've fallen flat on her face if Trick wasn't holding onto her because she was shit-faced on whatever the fuck he gave her.

I pulled Bambi off me and took a step toward Trick. "The girl is barely old enough to bleed. Get her the fuck outta here, you stupid fuck!"

All eyes turned and stared. Someone dropped a bottle, and it crashed on the floor.

Trick looked down at the girl. "Zoe here doesn't have a curfew," he sneered. She started to cry.

Wrecker was there and pulled the girl away from Trick. "I'll call her a cab, Prez."

Trick's bloodshot eyes were full of hate and anger. The chip on his shoulder was just as big as mine. The same hatred I had for him consumed me for fucking years, even after I took over as chapter prez.

I moved, standing toe-to-toe with him, my fists clenching. "You still wear the Bastard patch, but you're not welcome here tonight."

"I didn't come here to party. Got something I wanna bounce off you."

I turned and sat on a couch, pulling Bambi onto my lap. "You bounce something off the whole club when I hold church. Not here. You're killin' my good buzz. Get out of my sight."

Trick shrugged his shoulders. "Well, then, I'll stay for the party." He turned and headed to the bar.

Dani stood there beside Lacey, her eyes wide from witnessing the whole thing. Bambi wiggled her ass on my lap, turning my cheek to look at her. "Relax, Heavy, and let Bambi make you feel good," she whispered.

I smiled and palmed her ass as I shoved my tongue into her mouth. She moaned, digging her nails into my shoulders as I held her there, raising my hips against her wet panties.

I looked over at Dani again, and her face turned beet red. She mouthed the words *Fuck you,* turned up her nose, and walked away with Lacey.

Hammer was having a killer time with the now topless Roxi on the other couch while she ground her hips on his lap. When another song came on the jukebox, I heard hoots and whistles. I turned to look over and saw Dani and Lacey touching each other as they danced right on the bar. Trick was standing at the far end, watching like everyone else.

It felt like a punch in the gut as I watched Dani lower herself and crawl on her hands and knees toward Trick. She sat on the edge of the bar and wrapped her thighs around his waist. Trick handed her a full shot glass. She tilted it up to her mouth, drinking down the shot, and arched her back, so her tits were right in his face.

Bambi yelped when I lifted her off my lap. I wasn't fast enough. I saw red. Blood red. I stormed over, shoving the prospect. Trick's hand shot out and grabbed Dani's tits in his filthy hands. She smacked him hard across the face. Lacey screamed when Trick backhanded Dani. She fell back on the bar, and Trick was on top of her.

I grabbed the back of his cut and hauled him off Dani. People moved away as I shoved him hard face-first into a bunch of barstools. He stumbled, catching himself before he fell. When he turned, I was on him. I swung and landed a hard jab to his mouth. He staggered back, and his lip was cut.

He wiped the blood on his forearm. "I lost fifty-god-damn-grand because of that little cunt years ago!" He came at me, shoving my back against the bar. He threw a good punch, smashing his fist to my nose. Roadkill was there, pulling him off me.

I stepped toward Trick as Roadkill held him back. I tasted blood and wiped some off my busted nose. "If you touch what belongs to me again, I'll kill you."

CHAPTER 11
DANI

REAPER BASTARDS

MC

WASHINGTON, D.C.

I was so fucking mad at Heavy watching him paw at the dark-haired club whore, that all I wanted to do was kick him in the dick. But instead, I decided to play his own damn game. I recognized the man Heavy just had words with. They called him Trick, and he was the club's president seven years ago. Anyone who saw their heated words about the young girl with him couldn't deny the hate they had for each other. When I saw him standing at the end of the bar watching me dance, I crawled to him—knowing Heavy was watching. But when I took the shot glass Trick offered me, he went too far by grabbing my tits like he was going to rip them off. So, I slapped him. The whole world spun when he backhanded me hard, and I fell back on the bar. Everything happened so fast as Heavy pulled him off me, and they threw punches at each other. When Roadkill came and pulled Trick off Heavy, Lacey was there, offering her hand to me.

"Trick is Heavy's father!" Lacey said as she helped me up to move away.

Heavy's father?

When it was over, Trick left, climbing on his bike and burning rubber as he peeled out of the clubhouse. Heavy and Roadkill came over to the other side of the bar, reaching up for Lacey and me. I lowered myself down and held onto Heavy's broad shoulders. He gripped my waist, lifting me off the bar and setting my feet on the cement floor. I watched as Roadkill held out his muscular arms. Lacey knelt down, wrapping her arms around his neck. He scooped her up in his arms and carried her off the bar, then set her down on her feet.

There was blood smeared on Heavy's face. Wrecker appeared, handing him a bandana to wipe the blood. "I called the girl a cab."

Heavy wiped some of the blood from his face as Wrecker walked away. His brows furrowed as he tilted my chin. "You okay?"

I blinked a few times. "He slapped me good, but yeah. I'm okay."

"You'll have a bruise in the morning. Trick's been hitting women for as long as I can remember."

I knew then why Heavy punched the wall at the Dollhouse instead of my face.

My throat burned as I choked back tears. "I saw that bitch touching your dick and slobbering all over you, and I was ready to claw her eyes out...and yours! I wanted to get the same reaction out of you and took the shot from Trick. Lacey just told me he's your father. Why didn't you tell me?"

"It didn't matter when you got on that bus seven years ago. I never expected you to come back." Heavy let go of my chin and gripped my hips, pulling me close to him. I wrapped my arms around his shoulders. "Hammer is having a good time with Roxi, and my brothers will make sure he's fed, fucked, and well-rested. Let's get on the bike and go home."

"Can Lacey bring my shopping bags over to your house tomorrow?"

"Sure."

I held onto Heavy tightly as he rode us back to his house. He sat me in the kitchen and filled a hand towel with ice cubes. He sat in the chair across from me and gently pressed the cool cloth to my cheek. "We're both gonna wake up with shiners in the morning."

I smiled. "I guess it's just part of the gig."

Heavy smiled then and chuckled low. I liked this side of him, as it brought out the gray of his eyes. Plus, he didn't look at me with that pissed-off glare for once. Then he leaned back in the chair, crossing his arms over his chest, and that severe stare came back. "My club stripped Trick of his prez patch a few years after I got you on that bus to AC. He was getting our chapter into a bunch of bad shit dealing with cartels and the Russian mob. He still wears the Bastards patch but holds the lowest rank in my chapter, only just above the prospects, which isn't something to be proud of. We hit him where it hurts...his pride. I took over as prez—the vote was unanimous—and Tye was kicked out and stripped of his patches. He's probably dead now, his body rotting in an unmarked grave somewhere. That's what he did with your friend, Krista. He was a worthless piece of shit, and so is my dear old dad."

My jaw hung open as I listened to Heavy. He stood from the chair and began to pace, looking like a caged panther. "Now that Trick knows you're here, he's going to come after you. He'll want to sell you into some sex-trafficking ring. Hell, I wouldn't put it past him to work with our enemy, the Bloody Aces."

I dropped the cloth on the kitchen table and stood in front of Heavy, stopping him from pacing. "I came back because I love you, Heavy."

He was quick, snaking his hand up the back of my neck. He fisted a handful of my hair and pulled. "It's dangerous to love a man like me, Danika. You'll end up damaged, broken, or dead."

"I'm already damaged, and I've been broken a few times over the years. But I know you'll keep me safe. Like you did before."

Heavy's mouth crashed onto mine, kissing me roughly. I dug my fingers into the leather of his cut, parting my lips and inviting his hungry tongue. I jumped, wrapping my thighs around his waist and my arms around his shoulders. He gripped my ass, carrying me to the kitchen table and set me down on it. He released me, and with one wave of his arm, shoved everything off the kitchen table onto the floor.

We kissed again, our tongues and lips frenzied and rushed as he undid the front of my jean shorts, yanking them down and dropping them to the floor. He unzipped the front of his jeans, shoving his briefs down and his hard, giant dick bounced against his hard stomach. I laid back on the table, spreading my thighs, my pussy slick and ready for him. I gripped the edge of the table as Heavy leaned over me. He gripped the front of my tank with both hands and ripped it open down the middle, then tugged my bra down, exposing my breasts.

"Your tits are gorgeous, Dani. I'm glad you didn't pump them with that fake shit," he said, his voice deep, as his warm hands brushed across both my nipples.

Heavy leaned down, capturing my right nipple with his mouth, sucking and licking, then swiping his tongue back and forth over it, teasing it. His lips and tongue moved to my left nipple, tormenting it just the same. He released it with a smack and stood, running his hand down my chest to my stomach, as it fluttered with anticipation, needing all of him.

He gripped his monster cock and rubbed the head up and down my wet slit. "Is this what you want, little slut?"

"Yes, please, Heavy!" I begged breathlessly.

He eased the head in slowly, then more, stretching me so wide, filling up my pussy. I reached down between my legs and felt that he was only halfway in. I gripped the table's edge tighter, my eyes wide. I was so wet, he slid the rest of himself in, and I cried out, feeling him up against my cervix.

He went still, his hooded eyes full of lust. "Relax, Dani. I'm big, but I'll go gentle."

I nodded and whimpered as he gently pulled out and eased his way back in. Our eyes were locked with one another, his hands brushing across my tits, lightly pinching my nipples.

He kept his pace slow as he groaned. "You're so tight. Just the perfect fit for me."

I closed my eyes, enjoying the pleasure of him and moaned again. "Faster, Heavy."

He grabbed my wrists, pinning them down at my sides, and thrust into me faster. He reached down and pressed the pads of his fingers gently on my swollen clit. As he rubbed small circles over and over, I suddenly cried out with an exhilarating orgasm. My walls pulsated around his massive rod. He leaned his head back and pumped into me a few more times, then pulled out. His cock was slick with my wetness and he gripped it and pumped it a few times. His white-hot cum squirted, landing on my breasts and stomach.

CHAPTER 12
DANI

REAPER BASTARDS

MC

WASHINGTON, D.C.

It sounded fake when Dani said that she loved me because I'd never heard a chick tell me that before. But when she looked at me with those amber-colored eyes, I got fucking lost in them. I wanted to hurt her, feed her some pain to show her I wasn't the kind of man who loved anything or anyone. But then when I was deep inside her pussy, I saw the young teenage Danika I remembered from years ago. I didn't want to hurt her. I wanted to make her feel good and see that fire in her eyes. I would've fucked and busted a load all over Dani again early that morning, but I knew her tight pussy would be sore. She needed to get used to my size. I lay in the bed with her until she fell asleep. She mewed like a cat, and her brows scrunched together when I climbed out of bed. I took a quick shower and looked at my reflection in the steamed bathroom mirror. Trick landed a good one—a dark bruise was forming underneath both my eyes.

I swung a leg over my bike and rode back to the clubhouse. It was deserted when I pulled in through the bay doors and parked next to Wrecker's bike. The clubhouse was littered with beer cans and bottles, along with cigarette butts and black skid marks all over the cement floor. The place smelled like weed and burnt rubber.

I scanned the whole clubhouse to see Wrecker lying on one of the pool tables with a naked chick sleeping beside him. Roadkill sat at the bar with his forehead lying on top of his forearms. I walked up, slapping a hand on his shoulder. "You still breathing, brother?"

He raised his head, shaking it. "Fuck," was all he could mutter.

I sat on the stool next to Roadkill and grabbed the half-empty pack of Marlboro's on the bar. I pulled out a lighter from my pocket and lit one. "Where's Hammer?"

"Roxi took him back to her place," Roadkill grumbled, then laid his forehead back down.

Wrecker rose from the dead, sitting up and groaning on the pool table. He rolled the naked chick off his lap and climbed off the pool table. He was still shit-faced, staggering over to sit on a barstool beside me. He looked at my busted-up face and shook his head. "How's Danika? Hope her face ain't as ugly as your mug."

"We put some ice on her cheek, but she'll still bruise." I took a long drag off the cigarette and exhaled. "Now that Trick's seen Dani, he'll try and take her. She won't be safe...not here, at least."

"You can fool everyone and even yourself, Heavy—but you can't fool me. You liked Dani years ago. That's why you put her on a bus to get out of DC. You knew if Trick got ahold of her, she would've disappeared with a bunch of Russian sex-slave traders. She'd probably be dead now too. But you saved her. She's safer with the club than out on her own. Just cause you have Trick's blood running through your veins doesn't mean shit; it's just fucking DNA, brother." Wrecker grabbed my shoulders. "You're not Patrick Stone. You're Hendrix Stone, the President of the Reaper Fucking Bastards. Trick is just as slimy as those goddamn Bloody Aces. He doesn't live by our club's code. Why don't you slap a property patch on the girl and claim her as your old lady? She'll have the highest rank among all the other old ladies and be protected by every member of our club and all the other chapters."

Wrecker knew me more than anyone else in the club; he was my brother from another mother. He was the only one who could get away with laying all the cards on the table and telling me straight off the cuff.

"Dani, Lacey, and Roxi are set to shoot the film next week with Hammer. We're still gonna make bank with this film. And I'm not going to disappoint."

"Is this what Dani wants to do? Or is it something you're making her do?"

I dropped the cigarette and crushed it out with my boot heel. "I'm making her do it to punish her. She's gonna regret ever stepping foot into the Dollhouse and back in Reaper Bastards territory."

I slapped Wrecker on the shoulder. "Let's go find Trick."

"It's only three a.m. He usually hangs at the Cherry Pie titty bar."

I climbed off the stool and looked over at Roadkill. His forehead was still on his forearms, and he was snoring like a bear. "He's not a Reaper Bastard anymore, and we're taking his cut."

Wrecker and Roadkill rode with me, and we found Trick's bike parked outside the Cherry Pie. The bartender, Diamond, rushed over to the end of the bar when we entered. "Trick's in the second VIP room with Sadie and Mandy. That asshole is shit-faced and getting rough with the girls. He's been here for hours!"

Roadkill pulled a revolver from inside his cut as we walked down the dark narrow hallway to VIP Room 2. Roadkill hiked his leg and kicked in the door. It flew open, busting a hole in the wall. The girls screamed and ran past us and out of the room as we walked in.

Trick stood from the couch when Roadkill stepped up, raised the gun, and pointed it between his eyes.

Trick smiled at Roadkill. "I have a pussy for a son because he's not man enough to pull the trigger himself."

I moved to Roadkill and pressed his hand that held the gun down to his side. "You're already a dead man. We're taking your cut. You're not a Reaper Bastard anymore."

Trick shrugged his old and tattered cut, turned it around, and spit on the center patch—the skull wearing a crooked crown.

He tossed it to me. "I don't need the Reaper Bastards. There's plenty of other clubs out there with colors I'd be proud to wear on my back, son."

I handed Trick's cut to Wrecker, then threw a right hook, smashing my knuckles into Trick's jaw. He stumbled back, falling on the couch, blood spewing from his mouth. I was on him, pounding both my fists one after another into his eyes, then his mouth.

Wrecker pulled me off him. "Come on, Heavy; let's go."

Trick was knocked out cold.

I shoved Trick's cut into my saddlebag, and the three of us rode back to the clubhouse. We called every chapter member for church, and an hour later, they were all there. Roadkill started up a blazing fire in a rusty trash barrel.

I held up Trick's cut as I looked into the eyes of every one of my brothers. "Starting today, Patrick Stone, aka Trick, is no longer a Reaper Bastard. He will never be protected by the club, nor will he have our respect. He will never be allowed to step inside this clubhouse again. He is dead to me, and he's dead to all of you, my Reaper Bastard brothers."

I tossed Trick's cut into the fire, and the Reaper Bastards watched until it was burned to ash.

I left the clubhouse and went back to my house. I couldn't get enough of Dani, and all I thought about on the ride home was fucking her in every tight hole.

When I entered my house, I found Dani in the living room. Her wet, dark-brown hair was combed back, and she was wrapped in a bath towel. She sat on the couch, rummaging through one of the dozen or so shopping bags strewn on the coffee table and on the floor.

Her eyes lit up, and she smiled. The bruise started to show on her right cheek. "Lacey came by just now and dropped off my shopping bags."

My dick was hard all of a sudden seeing Dani like that—clean and naked under that towel. I stepped over some of the bags and got down on my knees. I pushed her thighs apart and moved myself in between them.

She gasped, her eyes going wide when I yanked the towel open. I leaned down and ran my tongue up between her soft pussy lips. She cried out, digging her fingers into my hair when I hiked her thighs up over my shoulders and slid my tongue into her wet hole. Her bald pussy was so goddamn soft and smelled so good.

"Heavy! Oh my god!" was all she could say when I started flicking my tongue back and forth over her clit. I wrapped my lips around it and sucked nice and gentle while I slid 2 fingers up her tight, wet hole. She tasted so fuckin' sweet, making my dick so hard it hurt.

Dani ran her hands through my hair, and her head fell back while she moaned and whimpered. Her sweet ass squirmed as she rode my mouth. I looked up to watch her pretty tits jiggle and sway. I kept up the pressure, sucking on her clit, then flicked it until she screamed my name, her wet juices squirting all over my mouth and beard.

I rose, unzipping my jeans, and shoved them down with my briefs. Dani's eyes were closed, and she was breathing fast. I flipped her over and spanked her ass before I shoved half my dick inside her soaked pussy.

I eased out and pushed back in just a bit more each time, stroking my fingers up and down her back to help her relax and get used to my tight fit. She gripped the couch pillows, and she moaned. "I love how you go easy with me."

"I wanna make you feel good like you make me feel, Dani," I grunted while I fucked her nice and steady.

Both our bodies were covered in sweat, and my throbbing dick was about to explode. I couldn't hold back much longer listening to Dani moan and cry out my name, begging me to fuck her faster.

"I'm on the pill, Heavy. I need to feel you come inside me!" Dani screamed, and that was music to my ears. I pumped into her a few more times and shot my hot load deep inside her.

CHAPTER 13
DANI

REAPER BASTARDS

 MC

WASHINGTON, D.C.

I went with Lacey to see her doctor, and we both tested clean a few days before the shoot. Heavy dressed in a T-shirt, jeans, and boots, but didn't wear his Reaper Bastards cut since he drove us in his truck, telling me that, *"Bastards don't wear cuts while driving a cage."* It was noon when we arrived at the MGM. I'd been in all the casinos in Atlantic City, but this was the first time I'd ever stepped into a high-dollar suite. I overheard Heavy talking to Wrecker that a man named Nolan Reynolds ran all the business in and out of the MGM casino. I wondered if I'd ever get to meet him.

The suite was enormous with a bar loaded with unopened bottles of top-shelf liquor, a long sectional couch in the living room, and a separate bedroom with two, king-sized beds. I saw Lacey first and walked over to the bar where she stood behind it, pouring herself a glass of wine. She was dressed in a pretty pink satin robe with flowers on it and a pair of hot pink stilettos. Her eyes were glassy, and her eyelids were half-closed as she batted her false lashes and smiled at me. I could tell she was on something—weed, meth, or both. Roxi was there, too, sitting on a barstool dressed in a black satin robe. Her long, fiery-red hair had wavy curls, and her green eyes sparkled as she sipped on a glass of wine. She was businesslike and polite at the clubhouse party, but I didn't feel that friendly warmth as I did with Lacey.

Roxi introduced me to her friend and hairdresser, Anna. "Anna did Lacey's and my hair and makeup. She'll get you all dolled up before we get in front of the camera."

Just then, Wrecker and Roadkill entered the suite with Hammer.

"Welcome, my Bastard brother!" Heavy said as they approached, giving Hammer a bear hug. Hammer steered his eyes over to us girls.

"The three of you ladies look fabulous!" he said, rubbing his palms together as his smiling eyes roamed down our bodies with approval. But his eyes steered back to Roxi as she batted her long lashes at him.

Wrecker sat on a stool at the bar. "Hey Brace—I mean, Lacey, make a drink for us, would ya? Any of that real expensive shit that's back there."

Lacey smiled, her starry eyes only lit up for him. "Sure, Wrecker!" She reached for a bottle of bourbon and struggled with opening the wax-covered cork. The bottle crashed onto the marble-tiled floor. The glass shattered, splashing liquor everywhere. Her bottom lip trembled. "I'm so sorry! I'm such a stupid klutz."

Roadkill was there suddenly, towering over Lacey's small frame. His eyes scanned her body, then he offered his hand out to her. "Step around the glass." He grumbled low. That was only the second time I'd ever heard him say more than two words since I saw him almost rip Big Bobby's head off at the Dollhouse.

Lacey raised her head to reveal tear-filled eyes. She placed her small hand into his bear-like palm, and he walked her to the couch so she could sit down. I came to sit next to her, wrapping my arm around her shoulder. "Are you okay, Lacey?"

"Yeah, I'm okay," she sniffled. She leaned close, whispering in my ear. "Wrecker doesn't want me because of my ugly braces."

Roadkill turned and stormed out the door of the suite. That man was not just scary; he was so damn weird! Did he like Lacey?

I wrapped my arms around her. "Well, he's just a stupid oaf like all men are," I whispered back to her. I wanted to knee Wrecker in the balls for hurting Lacey's feelings. "Did you get high before you came here today, Lacey?"

She leaned away and sniffled. "Yeah. I smoked a joint and took some Xanax. I've never starred in a porn film before. I'm a bit nervous today."

Heavy approached us after telling Wrecker to go find out what was up with Roadkill. I looked up at him as Lacey wiped her nose with the sleeve of her robe.

"You okay, Lacey?" he asked. It just sounded so hollow, like he really didn't care.

"No, she's not," I said. "She's never been in a film before. She's not ready."

"She can sit out this time. It'll just be you and Roxi with Hammer."

Wrecker walked back into the suite. "Roadkill said he's heading down to the casino."

Heavy shook his head. "He knows he shouldn't sit at the roulette table. He'll lose several grand in the next fucking hour. Call and get someone to clean up the glass." He turned and told me to follow him.

I stood from the couch to let Lacey put her feet up and lay down. Roxi, Hammer, and I followed Heavy into the bedroom.

We met the film director, Stanley Kane. He was a tall, good-looking man with a very dark tan. He was all businesslike, telling us three to be aware of where the camera is at all times while we performed whatever positions he wanted us in. He said the lighting was really good in the room and that he'd shoot us on the one bed first. Then we would pose for still shots. He also went into detail about how he wanted to get Hammer's cum shot on film.

I sat in a chair in the bathroom with Anna while she did my makeup and put a curling iron to my hair, giving it thick wavy curls. I undressed and changed into the outfit Heavy picked out as his favorite for the shoot—a red lace push-up bra and panties that matched the red lipstick that Anna applied to my lips.

When I entered the bedroom, Wrecker and Heavy were sitting on a couch. Heavy smiled at me with approval, but I was hoping for his death glare full of jealousy. Did it really not bother him to watch me suck on Hammer's dick in front of him and everyone else in the room? All week Heavy was so gentle and caring when we fucked in every room of his house. He would hold me as we lay in my bed, but then he'd leave me in the middle of the night to sleep in his bed alone.

Hammer stood beside the bed. He was shirtless then but still wore his jeans. He started to kiss Roxi, running his hands over her naked body. Stanley directed me to get on the bed and undo Hammer's jeans to suck his dick. When he began shooting, I crawled on my hands and knees across the bed as Hammer licked on Roxi's nipples.

Hammer looked down at me as I sat to unzip his jeans. His dick was big and hard as a rock when I pulled it out. I stroked his full length with my hands and batted my eyes up at him. He groaned, shoving his thumb in my mouth.

I couldn't see Heavy as my back was turned, but I could feel his stare burning right through me.

I climbed off the bed as Stanley shouted, "Cut!"

I stormed out of the bedroom, through the living room and out the door of the suite.

My face collided into a big burly chest dressed in a suit jacket. I looked up to see the large man who'd grabbed me by my arms. He had dark eyes and a beard. His body was massive!

"You should put some clothes on, Miss. You can't walk around the casino like this," he said in a deep voice.

"What the fuck, Danika!" Heavy's gruff voice came from behind me. I turned around to see that all-too-familiar look of rage in his eyes.

"Hey, Brody, good to see ya." Heavy approached, slapping the big man on the shoulder. "You comin' in to watch the shoot?"

The man named Brody chuckled. "No, dude. That's all for your entertainment. I just wanted to swing by to see if you and your brothers needed anything. And Nolan Reynolds sends his regards."

"Thanks. The suite is a bit too fancy, but it's a great location to shoot some good scenes for the film."

The men exchanged bro hugs, and then Brody left us, walking back down the long hallway to the elevator.

Heavy wrapped a thick white robe over my shoulders. "What the fuck was that all about?"

I growled at him as I slid my arms into the robe and closed it. "You really don't care, do you?"

"Care about what?"

"That I was about to suck another man's dick right in front of you!"

He groaned, rubbing both hands down his face. "It's just part of the gig, Dani. I'm not the jealous type. This is business."

Images like snapshots invaded my mind just then—my stepfather raping me, hurting me, shaming me, shattering me. Something snapped inside me, and the floodgates of emotion came gushing out. I screamed, grabbing fistfuls of my hair. "Don't make me do this! I can't anymore! I'll run away!" I crumpled to the floor sobbing as I rocked back and forth at Heavy's feet.

He knelt, pulling me into his strong arms, rubbing his warm hands on my back. "Shh, Danika. You're safe. You don't have to do anything. Just sit right here and let it all out."

CHAPTER 14
HEAVY

REAPER BASTARDS

 **MC**

WASHINGTON, D.C.

I sat in the hallway and held Dani's trembling body in my arms as she cried. When she quieted down to whimpers and hiccups, I pulled her off the floor with me. Her eyes were puffy, and she wiped her nose with the sleeve of the fancy robe.

I cupped her face in my hands and kissed her on the lips. "Stay here. I'll get your bag and tell Wrecker I'm taking you back to the house."

I headed back into the suite while Dani leaned up against the wall, tying the robe closed.

Wrecker was standing there when I walked in, holding Dani's bag. He rubbed the back of his neck and handed me her bag. "Is she okay, brother?"

"No. She needs to let out some bad shit from her past. I'm taking her back to the house, and I'll come back. Stanley will just have to shoot some scenes with Hammer and Roxi."

"I got this, Prez. I'll take Lacey home after the shoot and check on Roadkill. Just stay with her."

I hugged Wrecker, slapping him hard on the back. "Thanks, brother."

I took Dani down the elevator to the parking garage and got her in the truck. She was quiet on the ride home. She looked so small in that big white robe, staring out the passenger window. Once inside the house, I took her hand and led her to my bedroom. She climbed into the bed while I kicked off my boots, then I got in and held her.

"Do you want to tell me what he did to you? I get it if you don't wanna talk about it."

Dani clung to me, and this is what she told me:

She never felt love from her mother growing up. The only grown-up who showed her any kindness or care was her dad, whom she barely remembered. When she was five years old, she could remember her mom and dad getting drunk and high, throwing things, and yelling at each other. The men dressed in blue and black police uniforms came and talked to her with smiles. Some of them would ask her about the Dora the Explorer doll she carried with her everywhere. The policemen handcuffed her dad and took him away in a police car. As a little girl, she wondered why it was her dad, who was made to go away in the police car and not her mom. This happened more times than Danika could count, and then one day, her dad was gone. Danika's mom told her he was never coming back because he found out that Danika wasn't really his daughter. She was told she was a mistake and that her mom didn't know who her real father was.

Her mom dated lots of men as Danika was growing up. When she was thirteen, her mom met Larry Hodges. Danika's mom said she finally hit the jackpot catching a man with a real job, who didn't beat her like all the other loser men she had in her bed. Larry seemed nice at first and gave both Danika and her mom attention and kindness. Sometimes when Danika missed the bus, Larry would drop her off at school on his way to work.

But then things started getting weird when she was going through puberty. There were times that Danika caught Larry staring at her chest or her legs with lustful eyes. Larry gave her more hugs to the point he got one from her every single day. They made her cringe as his hands lingered on her body. She began to believe it was her fault because Larry told her she was much prettier than her mom. He planned to take her shopping for pretty clothes when he got his next bonus check from work.

Danika's hateful mom could also see how Larry looked and touched her. She became jealous of her own daughter, screaming at Danika, *"Larry would rather fuck a little whore like you than his own wife!"*

Larry Hodges raped Danika for the first time on her 15th birthday. She was a virgin and couldn't tell her mom for fear she would get beaten or kicked out of the house. Larry made a deal with Danika—that he would protect her from her mom's cruelty as long as she kept this secret they shared. That she didn't have to worry about getting pregnant because Larry had an operation to fix that. The man knew what to say to make Danika feel safe. He was always gentle, saying the right words Danika wanted to hear and buying her nice things. For years he climbed into her bed at night and touched her body any chance he could get without being caught by her mom. Danika knew she wasn't his first victim because he seemed so confident in the way he manipulated and abused her. Larry was living a good life, knowing he was able to fulfill his disgusting appetite for preying on young girls to satisfy his sexual needs.

Danika saved five hundred dollars working part-time at the local consignment shop. She graduated from high school with a 3.9 grade point average. On her eighteenth birthday, Danika packed her backpack with clothes, climbed out of her bedroom window, and ran away. She escaped the monster who preyed on her for years. It was the same night she met me seven years ago.

"You put me on a bus that same night and saved me from a fate far worse than I had just escaped from Heavy." Dani finished telling her story, her voice sounding so far away.

I cupped Dani's cheek and looked into her tear-soaked eyes. "My name is Hendrix. Hendrix Stone."

Dani didn't tell me anymore, so I just held her in my arms until we both fell asleep together in my bed.

Larry Hodges was a middle-aged, heavyset man with brown hair that grayed at his temples. His eyes fluttered open, only to suddenly realize he was lying face down and naked on a bed in a shitty motel room that smelled like piss. His hands were bound behind his back with duct tape. He couldn't open his mouth because it was duct-taped shut. He turned his face and saw me sitting in a chair with one ankle over my other knee while Roadkill stood next to me. Then he saw the big black man standing so close beside the bed looking down at him.

The duct tape muffled whatever it was Larry was trying to say.

"Hello, Larry," I said. "Your heart is racing so fast—like you're running a fucking marathon right about now. And you're wondering why you're naked and tied up on a bed in a piss-smelling, roach-infested motel room. Do you remember Danika Stevens?"

Larry's eyes went wide, shaking his head and mumbling against the duct tape.

"Oh, come on, Larry, how could you forget a pretty girl like her? She was your stepdaughter."

He shut his eyes and nodded his head.

"Danika told me everything. How you raped her when she was a virgin at just fifteen."

Larry began to cry, and tears ran down his cheeks while he shook his head. Roadkill lit up a joint as I told Larry what was going to happen next.

I nodded to the black man. "I want you to meet my friend here, Tiny Tyrone. His little sister was raped and killed by some sick—and now dead—piece of shit just like you."

Tyrone started to undress, pulling his triple extra-large T-shirt over his head.

"It's kind of a joke...we call him Tiny Tyrone, but he's not tiny."

Tyrone unzipped his jeans and shoved them down along with his boxers. Then out came his dick—all ten inches of it. He wasn't even hard yet. Tyrone spat in his big palm and started to jerk himself off while staring down at Larry's naked ass.

Tyrone licked his bottom lip when his dick started to get harder and bigger. Larry started up his muffled screams behind the duct tape again. Tyrone walked over to the end of the bed and climbed on it. He snatched Larry's ankles and spread them wide apart, then moved closer to the crack of Larry's ass.

"You're getting ready to feel what it's like to be raped, Larry Hodges. Tyrone is going in dry and fucking your asshole with that giant black dick of his."

Roadkill handed me the joint and I took a long hit when Tyrone went to work, spreading Larry's ass cheeks and grabbing his hips. Larry's screams didn't reach any ears outside the motel room when Tyrone rammed half his dick inside Larry's tight asshole. He pulled out and thrust all of that big black dick inside this time while spanking Larry's ass over and over again. Roadkill whipped out his phone and took a few photos for souvenirs.

It took thirty minutes while Roadkill and I caught a buzz off the weed before Tyrone shot a full load of cum into Larry's bleeding asshole. Tyrone climbed off the bed and went into the bathroom to take a shower.

I stood from the chair and walked over to the bed, where Larry blubbered on behind the duct tape. I pulled out my phone, grabbed a handful of Larry's sweat-dampened hair, and snapped a few photos. I clenched my jaw, baring my teeth. "I'm Heavy, the President of the Reaper Bastards MC. I know where you live, what you eat, and when you shit. If you touch another girl again, I'll send my sergeant, Roadkill, to pay you a visit. He likes to play doctor and will cut your dick and balls off with his surgical tools."

I inhaled hard, forcing snot up the back of my throat and spit a load in Larry's eye.

CHAPTER 15
DANI

REAPER BASTARDS

 MC

WASHINGTON, D.C.

We slept together in his bed ever since I told him about my past. Within a few weeks, I saw a different side of Heavy, or maybe it was Hendrix. He was like Jekyll and Hyde. He didn't give me that death stare anymore and was a little kinder to me.

Stanley shot some good scenes with Roxi and Hammer that weekend at the MGM. Hammer rode back home with a grin on his face, and he couldn't wait to talk about his new porn-star life to their Cleveland Chapter brothers. Roadkill lost five grand in the casino. Heavy told me he had a few too many bad habits he couldn't kick. One of them was gambling.

Heavy was no knight in shining armor; he was far from it. Heavy was a bad man, a dangerous outlaw, and a Reaper Bastard. Vengeance was justice in his world. I had to hold down the bile that threatened to rise from my throat when I looked at the photos on Heavy's phone. It was Larry Hodges naked and bound with duct tape. I could see the whites of his eyes and imagined his muffled screams of pain behind the tape while the big black man raped his asshole.

Heavy swiped his phone screen, showing more pictures of Larry and his bloody ass. "Tyrell's dick measures ten inches. That's before he gets it hard. He pounded into Larry's ass for a good half hour. Once we cut the duct tape, he got dressed, and we let him go. He drove home with a bloody asshole full of Tyrell's load. Roadkill will check in on Larry from time to time and cut his dick and balls off if he ever touches another girl again."

I was relieved and thrilled when Heavy offered me a job working at the Dollhouse. I didn't have to dance, only bartend and wait tables, plus I could keep every penny of my tips. On my first day at work, Heavy introduced me to the head bartender, Chasidy, who'd been working there for five years. She was straight-up and never fed Heavy any bullshit.

Chasidy never fucked any of the Reaper Bastards and told me it's just business for her at the Dollhouse. "My pussy gets enough good dick elsewhere," she said.

I liked her instantly, and Heavy respected her as a business associate. Chasidy took me under her wing and trained me. She gave me all the info I needed to know about each dancer and some of the regular customers and their favorite drink. Heavy only trusted his prospects to be the bouncers, and Teddy, who carried my shopping bags, worked on most nights. Sometimes when the weather was nice, groups of men would go play a round of golf and then come to the Dollhouse to drink and watch the girls dance. Some of them were just college boys, and some were middle-aged men, the rich CEO types who had a wife, as well as a girlfriend, and even some grandkids. Some of these men were kept on a tight leash at home, so when it was time to hang out with their buddies, they really let loose. Chasidy told me to watch those types because they would get too touchy-feely with not only the dancers but bartenders and waitresses too.

It was a Saturday night when a group of those rich men dressed in expensive golf shirts and khaki shorts walked into the Dollhouse while I worked the bar with Chasidy. The men ordered a round of beers and whiskey shots. Jasmine was dancing on stage and around the pole. She was a very petite Vietnamese girl with small breasts who fit into a pair of size one jeans. The golfers were having a good time sliding bills into Jasmine's G-string, whistling and clapping, as she performed on the pole. Lacey was next to step on the stage. Her body was toned and lean, and I loved to watch her perform on the pole. That night she wore her white, thigh-high stripper boots and hot pink pasties on her nipples. She danced to the song "Pony" by Ginuwine, while gracefully performing back hook spins, boomerang, and cradle spins.

I slid a beer across the bar to a customer when the table of golfers erupted with drunken laughter. I looked up to see Lacey snatching up her dress and rushing off the stage to the dressing room behind the black velvet curtains.

Chasidy stood beside me and saw what happened too. She shook her head. "Those suit and tie assholes probably said something cruel about her braces."

"They're lucky to sit there and watch a gorgeous woman like Lacey perform for them," I replied when Lacey walked up to the bar. She wore a bright orange skintight minidress, and her nipples poked through the thin material. She sat on the stool in front of Chasidy and me.

"Can you pour me a screwdriver, Dani?" she asked me.

I smiled and placed my hand on top of hers with long nails painted with white polish. "Of course, babe. It's on the house."

I made the drink with a mix of orange juice and vodka. When I handed it to Lacy, I leaned across the bar. "Did those assholes say something shitty to you?"

Tears welled in her eyes. "The one in the pink button-down shirt told me to get off the stage. He said my ugly grill was blinding them."

I handed her a bar napkin when she began to cry. I looked over at the table and saw the man in the pink shirt. He looked older than the other men—in his late fifties—with a booming laugh and loud voice.

Just then, Roadkill entered the Dollhouse. His eyes steered right to Lacey as she wiped her tears and sipped on the screwdriver. He was there in the next second, standing next to her. He towered over Lacey, and I could see his jaw twitch when he spoke to her in a deep gruff voice. "Did someone hurt you?"

Lacey began to cry again, sniffling into the napkin.

My mouth curved up into a smile. "Yeah, Roadkill."

His eyes pivoted to me.

I nodded my head toward the front of the stage where the men sat. "That sharp-dressed man in pink over there just said something shitty to Lacey. Her feelings are hurt."

The three of us watched as Roadkill charged over to the table with quick strides. He reached down and gripped the man in the pink shirt by the throat and started punching him over and over in the face with quick jabs. The other men jumped out of their chairs, and the table and beer bottles fell, crashing on the floor. One of the younger men jumped on Roadkill's back and tried to pull him off the pink-shirt man.

"There's five of them against Roadkill! They'll hurt him!" Lacey cried out.

I wasn't the least bit worried about Roadkill because he could've killed all of them if he wanted to.

The prospect, Teddy, came over and joined the fight with Roadkill, taking down the man who jumped on Roadkill's back. By then, the pink-shirt man's face was a bloody mess when all the men headed toward the door. That's when Heavy and Wrecker walked in.

Heavy looked over at the broken chairs and broken beer bottles near the front stage. He crossed his tatted arms across his chest and shook his head while Wrecker chuckled. "Pull out the wallets, assholes. Hand over all your cash, plus one credit card to my fine-as-fuck bartender Dani over here. She'll make sure to leave my dancers and servers a nice big tip too."

The men groaned as they pulled out wallets from their khakis when Heavy called out to me, "Charge a grand to each card, darlin'."

I came from around the bar, and each of them handed me wads of cash and credit cards. I placed some of the cash in the register and handed some to Chasidy. I keyed in a thousand dollars from each credit card, then gave them back to the men.

"You white-collar cunts made a huge mistake coming into my club and trashin' it all up. You're lucky to be walking out alive. Don't ever come back or set foot in Reaper Bastards territory, or your bitch wives will become widows."

Roadkill came over to my side of the bar and grabbed a clean rag to wipe the blood off his knuckles. Lacey jumped off the barstool and walked over to him. Even though she wore high-heeled boots, she looked so tiny standing in front of him. She hesitated for a moment, then reached up and wrapped her arms around his neck. "Thanks, Roadkill."

He placed his big hands on her waist, bending down a little.

"Just hate seein' you cry," he grumbled as his long beard brushed along her bare shoulder.

I went over to start cleaning up the mess the assholes left behind when Heavy snared me around my waist. I knew he liked the leopard print booty shorts I wore with half my ass cheeks hanging out of them.

He gave my ass one hard smack, then sat down in a chair, planting me on his lap. He was all smiles when I wrapped my arms around his shoulders. "Do you need to spank my ass *that* hard?!"

He snaked his hand up underneath my leg and reached my ass, rubbing it. "Sorry, darlin'. I'll kiss it and make it feel better."

I arched a brow. "Something's not right. You never apologize."

He chuckled as he squeezed my thigh. "You and Chasidy can close the Dollhouse early tonight. We're throwing a party over at the clubhouse."

Thirty minutes later, Chasidy locked the front doors of the Dollhouse, and I climbed on the back of Heavy's bike. Roadkill pulled out a helmet from his saddlebag for Lacey, and she climbed on his bike. We rode in a tight group to the clubhouse. Hard rock music blared from the jukebox as bottle caps were twisted off beers, shots of whiskey and tequila were passed around, along with lit joints. Heavy and Wrecker, plus a few other Reaper Bastards, sat on the couches smoking joints and drinking beers. I sat on Heavy's lap, taking a hit off the joint he held. Wrecker had the petite Jasmine on his lap. She giggled, as she combed her small fingers through his dark beard, chatting away in her choppy Vietnamese accent.

Lacey sat next to Roadkill at the bar. She seemed to be doing all the talking, emphasizing with a wave of her long-manicured nails. Roadkill just sat there, straight-lipped with no emotion, and listened to every word that came out of her mouth.

Heavy's dark gray eyes were glassy as he smirked, pulling me closer. When we kissed, I swiveled my hips, and my ass pressed down on his lap. I felt his big dick hardening as his tongue pushed through my lips, and I moaned. All of a sudden, he pulled away and lifted me off his lap. He grabbed my hips, spun me around to face the bar, and smacked me hard on the ass again.

"Ow! Damnit, Heavy! I'm gonna have bruises all over my ass again!"

He chuckled. "Good way to mark you as mine, Tadpole. Now go get me another beer."

I huffed, arching my brow at him. It was so weird to hear him call me that after seven long years. I walked over to Chasidy, who was helping out behind the bar, and she handed me a cold bottle of beer. When I turned to walk back to Heavy, he was standing from the couch and holding a black leather vest with three patches sewn on the back that read:

Property of Heavy

I dropped the beer bottle, and it shattered on the cement floor.

Someone turned off the jukebox.

Wrecker lifted Jasmine off his lap and stood. "Shut the fuck up, all you filthy Reaper Bastards! Your Prez's got something to say to Dani!"

Heavy still had that devilish smirk on his face as he sauntered toward me with the vest. "Dani Storm, will you wear this cut and be my old lady?"

I slapped my hands over my mouth, and tears welled up in my eyes. "Yes, Heavy. I'll be your old lady and wear this cut with pride."

Heavy turned the vest around, and I put it on. I twirled around in a circle as all the Reaper Bastards clapped, hooted, and whistled.

I jumped into Heavy's arms, wrapping my thighs around his waist, and kissed him.

I heard Wrecker's booming voice again. "Now, everyone clear outta here! The prez and his old lady need to consummate this unholy union and fuck their brains out in the clubhouse!"

I let go of Heavy and turned around to receive hugs from Lacey, Jasmine, and Chasidy, along with a few of the other old ladies. Heavy received hugs and slaps on his back from his club brothers. Everyone climbed on their bikes and revved their throttle. They burned rubber off their back tires, leaving behind plumes of smoke and skid marks on the cement floor.

My booty shorts were soaked through, anticipating the moment I'd have Heavy's huge cock inside me. But then I smiled and took his hand. "Come with me. There's something I've never done but always wanted to try."

I led him over to the pool tables, where I stood with my back against one of them. I slid the booty shorts down my legs and placed them on the table. Heavy bit his bottom lip as his eyes roamed down my body, then straight to my bare pussy and my legs in thigh-high black boots.

I wrapped my arms around Heavy's shoulders. "Put me on the table."

"I'm likin' this already," he said as he gripped my waist and lifted me onto the table.

I was on my knees while I shrugged off my new properties cut and laid it over the edge of the pool table for some extra padding. I laid down on my back, then hung my shoulders and head off the side.

Heavy's brows shot up, and I watched him step up to my face as he unzipped his jeans. My mouth watered when he pulled out and showed me his hard, thick cock.

"Are you okay upside down like that, Dani?" His voice was laced with concern.

"Yes. I can take more of you in my mouth this way." I reached out, grabbed the back of his thighs, and pulled him to me.

I opened my mouth as Heavy guided the thick head in first, then slowly slid more and more in. My throat was open wider to take more of him as I sucked. He planted his hands on the table, leaning in just a bit more. While I sucked his cock, he moaned and slid two thick fingers into my wet pussy. He was gentle, only giving me as much of him that I could take down my throat.

He pulled out of my wet mouth, and he stepped back. "Turn around and bring that tight wet pussy over here," he demanded.

I sat up, turned around, and laid back down on the table. I gripped the edge of the pool table and spread my thighs for him. He leaned down, kissing me as he thrust deep into my wet softness. His tongue licked along my neck as his hands tangled in my hair. I wrapped my arms around him, lifting my hips to meet his.

He looked at me with hooded eyes full of desire. "I love you, Dani."

I cried out with pleasure and desire when I heard Heavy say those words, enjoying the sensations as he exploded deep inside me.

CHAPTER 16
HEAVY

 MC

WASHINGTON, D.C.

I liked the way Dani looked wearing my properties, and I was really proud of her. She held the highest rank among the other old ladies in the club. As the weeks went by, Dani proved herself working days and sometimes late into the night at the Dollhouse. She helped Chasidy manage things at the bar, and when Wrecker fired one of the dancers with a bad meth habit, Dani put out a job ad, and we hired two new girls. She even talked Lacey into giving the girls some pole dancing lessons when the club was closed for business.

Stanley Kane sent me his director's cut of the porn film with Roxi and Hammer. *Hammered* was the title we gave it. It was produced under Reaper Bastards Video, and the DC chapter wired the money to Stanley. We slapped some still shots of Roxi and Hammer on a DVD box cover and sold the mass market to porn and sex toy shops all over the country. It was also uploaded to several popular internet porn sites with pay-to-watch subscriptions.

One night a few weeks after the clubhouse party, Dani came home from working a double shift at the Dollhouse. I wanted to fuck her when she climbed into bed, but she wasn't in the mood—acting all cranky. She told me she had period cramps and then rolled over to go to sleep. I pulled her up against my chest, feeling her soft ass against my dick, and fell asleep with her.

The next night I was at the clubhouse shooting pool with Wrecker while I waited for Dani to get off work and drive there in my truck.

When Wrecker racked another game of pool and I took my shot to break, in walked Bambi. She wore cut-off jean shorts with half her big ass hanging out as she strutted over to me.

"Hey, Heavy, how's it hangin'?" she asked, batting her fake lashes at me.

I titled my beer for a drink and watched Wrecker make his first shot at the table. "Don't fuck up my pool game, Bambi. Go twerk your ass over to Roadkill."

Bambi turned to look at Roadkill sitting alone on a stool drinking beer while he used a switchblade to carve something into the wood of the bar.

"He's a little freaky and kinda scares me," she said, while she pouted. Then she made the mistake of moving way too close to me. She rubbed her tits that bulged out of her tank along my arm. "Just because you got an old lady now doesn't mean you can't dip that big cock into *my* ass."

That's when I saw Dani come storming in through the bay door of the clubhouse. Bambi snaked her hand down to my crotch. I shook my head and said, "My old lady is going to kick your big ass," when Dani grabbed a fistful of Bambi's dark hair, "right about now."

Bambi screamed when Dani pulled her hair and tossed her against the wall. Wrecker started laughing, and my brother Bagger hollered, "Catfight!" hoping he'd see tits popping out of torn shirts.

Dani smashed her fist into Bambi's nose, then pounced on her like a wildcat, digging her nails down the side of her face.

"Get her off me!" Bambi screamed.

I snatched Dani around the waist, pulling her away.

Bambi staggered a bit, and her nose bled.

"Let me go, Heavy!" Dani shouted.

I kept a firm grip around her waist. "Don't kill her, Dani. I'm not in the mood to dig a hole and bury the dumb bitch."

I let Dani take in a few deep breaths before I released her. But she twisted her fists into the front of Bambi's skimpy tank top. "If you ever touch or even *look* at my old man again, I'll get Roadkill to cut your fucking tits off!"

Dani suddenly let her go and stepped back. She put her hands to her stomach, then threw up what she ate for lunch all over Bambi's face.

Dani's eyes went wide and slapped a hand over her mouth. I followed close behind as she ran out the bay door. I saw her bent over and hurling again.

"Did you get fucked up at the Dollhouse?" I asked when I caught up to her.

She rose and spun around. "No! I can't drink, you dumbass! I'm fucking pregnant!"

That p-word just didn't register in my brain. "What?"

"I'm pregnant, Hendrix! And yes, it's yours!" She started to pace back and forth, combing her hands through her dark hair and mumbling. "I missed a day and forgot to take my birth control pills. My period is late. I took one of those piss-on-a-stick tests at the Dollhouse today. Those things are pretty accurate."

"You're gonna have a baby? My baby?" I asked, feeling my buzz wearing off.

She stopped pacing, and tears spilled down her cheeks. "Yes."

I wrapped my arms around her legs and lifted her. She stopped crying and started to giggle when I twirled her around. "That's the coolest fucking thing you've ever told me, Dani Storm, other than saying you love me."

"I do love you, Hendrix. I'm so happy that you're happy about this."

I put her back down, pulled her into my arms, and kissed her.

"Holy shit! Your tits are gonna get fucking *huge*!" I teased.

She huffed. "My huge tits will be full to feed the baby, so keep your hands off them!"

CHAPTER 17
DANI

REAPER BASTARDS

 MC

WASHINGTON, D.C.

Lacey gave me the number of her doctor, Dr. Cheryl Heller, and I called her to make an appointment and scheduled the date to have my first sonogram in three weeks. Heavy's Reaper Bastard brothers congratulated him when he announced that we were having a baby. Lacey, Chasidy, and the girls at the Dollhouse were ecstatic, and with the help of the club's old ladies, plans were already in the works to throw me a baby shower. The Reaper Bastards MC and the Dollhouse Girls became my new family.

When I told Heavy that we'd be able to find out the sex of the baby, I could see how it made him worry when he'd stare off and brood sometimes. He told me he could handle having a boy and wanted to teach him to be a better man than he ever was. But Heavy was the president of an outlaw MC and having a daughter scared him more than anything he'd ever seen or lived through. That familiar dark side of him came out when he told me, "If a boy even looks at my daughter sideways, I'll scare him so bad he'll run home shitting in his fucking pants!"

The past few weeks were hard on me physically, though. I woke up nauseous before sunrise, running into the bathroom to puke my guts out. Then I'd climb back in bed and snuggle up next to Heavy's warm body. He did little things that I thought were sweet like laying his big hand on my stomach and telling me he hoped the baby would have the same color eyes as mine.

My crazy-prego hormones were all jacked up, along with having morning sickness. Heavy didn't want me to breathe in cigarette smoke or weed and made me quit working at the Dollhouse. He wanted me to stay home and take care of the baby and the house. I was okay with that too.

Heavy knew more about me than I knew about him, but after some time, he opened up to me about his past. Heavy's mother's name was Sheila. She left the young Hendrix when he was only seven years old. His father, Patrick, beat her relentlessly like it was some quota he had to meet every month. He threatened to kill Sheila so many times when he was high on meth or tripped out on PCP. Heavy didn't have many memories of Sheila, but he did feel loved by her. He didn't hate her for leaving because he knew Patrick would hunt her down if she took little Hendrix with her. Heavy did think about her often and hoped she was still alive and had a good, happy life. Patrick turned his hatred and violence toward young Hendrix, and he was beaten with his father's fists. This was Patrick's way of raising his son *not* to be a pussy. Hendrix was told that women were useless. The only thing they were good for was to make a profit or use them up and throw them away like trash.

Heavy grew up believing he was just like his father. He treated me badly when I came back into his world because he couldn't fathom the idea that he *did* have a heart and was capable of love. As for me, I had to fuck men who only wanted to take what they could from me. I did what I had to do to survive, and in return, I got clothed, fed, and a place to sleep.

We both endured abuse from cruel and vicious men who had no mercy.

I couldn't ever remember feeling happy. When I first met Heavy all those years ago, I never thought I'd see him again, let alone end up pregnant with his baby. Heavy no longer looked at me with that death stare of his. His eyes now lit up with desire, kindness, and love for me.

Some nights as we slept together in bed, I'd see our baby in my dreams and promised him or her that their mom and dad would always love them and be there for them no matter what.

The bedroom I used to sleep in was turned into a nursery, and I was giddy with excitement and started to decorate it in pastel colors with cute things for decorations. The baby was getting spoiled by the old ladies and girls from the Dollhouse before it was even born.

It was two weeks before my sonogram, and early morning, when I stood in the driveway while Heavy pulled the bike out of the garage. He was riding over to the MGM to meet with

Nolan. After he strapped his helmet on, he pulled me into his arms and grabbed a handful of my ass.

"I could fuck you again before I head over to the MGM," he said as he planted a kiss on my lips.

I slapped his hand that still held onto my ass cheek and kissed him back. "Tame that monster in your pants until you come back home to me later. Then I'll ride you reverse cow-girl style."

"Yeehaw!" Heavy shouted, then swung a leg over his bike, started it up, and rode away.

I felt a bit better that morning and was relieved that I didn't have to run to the bathroom to throw up for once. This put me in a better mood, and after taking a nice long shower, I called up Lacey to see if she wanted to go shopping for some baby things. I dressed in a plain tank, yoga pants, and a pair of flip-flops, and drove the truck a few miles to her house.

When Lacey greeted me at the door, we both laughed at the way we had dressed the same. Lacey was a natural beauty, and I thought she looked much prettier in her casual look instead of all dolled up with makeup and hair products. Her blonde hair was straight with less curl. She had a nice complexion with no blemishes to her fair skin and pretty blue eyes. She still had issues with her self-confidence because of the braces, and as much as her friends told her she had nothing to be self-conscious about, she struggled with it.

We sat in her living room to finish drinking the smoothie she made for her morning breakfast, and she filled me in on how the girls and Chasidy were doing at the Dollhouse.

I also figured it out on my own that Roadkill liked Lacey. Like, a lot!

I had to mention Roadkill to find out how she felt about him. "I saw you having a very deep conversation with Roadkill at the clubhouse that one night. You held his attention the whole time."

Lacey smiled, and her pretty blue eyes lit up. "I used to be afraid of Roadkill. He never really says much at all, and he's so huge! I'd catch him staring at me sometimes, and I know he watches me dance at the club when he's there. He's never once made a pass at me or requested a private dance in the VIP. But he was like a knight in shining armor when he beat that asshole up at the Dollhouse. I saw him in a new light afterward. I know he grunts like a bear sometimes, but I can look past the rough and menacing exterior and see that he's a fine-as-fuck good-looking man!"

My jaw dropped, and we both giggled like teenagers.

A loud crash. The sound of wood splintering as Lacey's front door flew open and slammed into the wall.

Trick stepped through the open doorway. He raised his arm and marched over to the couch with quick strides as another man entered the house. Lacey screamed, clinging to me.

Trick's eyes were bloodshot as he glared angrily at me. "You and the blonde bitch are going for a ride."

CHAPTER 18
HEAVY

REAPER BASTARDS

 MC

WASHINGTON, D.C.

The ride to National Harbor was all jacked up with traffic on the beltway. I pulled the bike into a gas station to fill up when my phone started to buzz in the fork bag. I pulled it out to see a text message from Trick.

I opened it.

The pain that hit my gut felt like a stab from a knife.

An image of Dani. Tears and the look of terror in her pretty brown eyes. The blade of a buck knife pressed to her throat.

The phone buzzed again, and Trick's name lit up the screen.

I pushed the green button. "You're a dead man."

Trick chuckled on the other end. "Not if I kill you first, son."

"Deal. I'm all yours. Let. Her. Fucking. Go."

"Sounds like a fair trade. But I also got the blonde bitch here too. Maybe I'll just keep that one."

"When and where?"

"Meet me at noon at my clubhouse. You got two hours. Bring all your Reaper Bastard brothers along, but no firearms. We'll do this the old-fashioned way with knives and anything else you can use to kill."

"Your clubhouse? Whose club did you patch in with already?"

"I'm not only patched in, I'm the motherfuckin' president of the Bloody Aces MC!"

I hung up on him.

I scrolled through my phone and called Wrecker. I told him that Trick took Dani and Lacey to the Bloody Aces MC's clubhouse and to get every Reaper Bastard to meet at our clubhouse in thirty minutes.

I climbed back on the bike and twisted the throttle wide open, passing cars at breakneck speed around the beltway. All the bikes were parked when I pulled into the clubhouse through the bay door. I kicked my stand down next to Roadkill's bike. All my brothers gathered together as they stood by the bar—Roadkill, Bagger, Kable, Defcon, Tusk, Gater, and the two prospects.

I swallowed the big lump in my throat when I hugged Wrecker.

"I just got off the phone with Nolan Reynolds," he said. "Told him to hold off the law within a fifty-mile radius around the Bloody Aces clubhouse from now until tomorrow. We're going to get Dani and Lacey back. Then I'm going to kill Trick myself. For all of us."

"No." Roadkill cut off Wrecker as he stood with our brothers. "Trick took Lacey, and she belongs to me. I get him first."

CHAPTER 19
DANI

REAPER BASTARDS

 MC

WASHINGTON, D.C.

Everything was happening so fast, like a horrible nightmare that you can only remember parts of when you wake up. My survival instinct kicked in, making my brain block out things like turning a light switch on and off. It was the only way I could endure the traumatic experience.

The patch on the front of Trick's cut read President, but I couldn't see the back to know who the MC was. The other man looked about the same age and size as Trick, but he was bald and had a long beard. He sauntered over and sat next to me on the couch. I flinched, then gasped when he jerked me closer to him. Lacey screamed when he pulled out a big knife and pressed the blade to my throat. Trick snapped a picture and then moved his thumbs on his phone to send it. I hugged

Lacey and listened when he called and spoke to Heavy. I knew then that they were the Bloody Aces MC.

After Trick spoke to Heavy, he told us that if we screamed or cried out for help, he would kill us both. I believed him. Lacey and I did as Trick said when we left the house with him and the other man. My stomach felt queasy as fear gripped me, and I almost passed out. But I was worried about Lacey. She was in shock—her eyes wide—and I was afraid she'd completely shut down.

Trick pressed the gun barrel against my side as he walked close beside me. The other man wrapped his arm around Lacey's waist as they walked ahead of Trick and me. As I looked at the man's Bloody Aces three-piece patch on his back, I remembered Heavy telling me they'd been enemies of the Reaper Bastards for years, and that he wouldn't put it past Trick to join them.

He leaned closer to Lacey's hair. "Damn, you smell good. You got nice tits too. Bet they cost you a lot. Call me Shanker, baby girl."

Lacey didn't respond and kept walking.

An old rusty van with gray primer paint was parked behind my truck. Trick opened the back doors, shoving us to climb in. We sat together on the dirty carpet that smelled like piss and mildew, then wrapped our arms around each other. I went numb as Lacey sobbed in my arms. I had a dreadful fear of losing my baby.

"They're going to kill us," Lacey whispered. "I don't want to die, Dani."

"We're not going to die, Lacey. Trick wants Heavy, not us. Heavy, Roadkill and all the Reaper Bastards are on their way," I whispered back, not believing my own words.

Trick drove the van while Shanker sat in the passenger seat. I could tell the van was on the interstate, but I didn't know if we were going north to Maryland, or south to Virginia.

After what felt like forever, Trick parked the van and pulled open the back doors. He pointed the gun at us while we climbed out. We were parked in front of an old, run-down warehouse with rusty siding. The emblem made of sheet metal above the bay door was the same as the center patch on Trick's and Shanker's cuts. This was the clubhouse that belonged to the Bloody Aces MC.

We entered through a side door to an empty warehouse. It was a shithole with no couches or bar or pool tables like the Reaper Bastard clubhouse. The cement floor was littered with trash, and the stench of piss made me swallow down bile. Four men stood around two wooden chairs. In the far corner of the warehouse, I saw an old mattress on the dirty floor, and a camera attached to a tripod stood a few feet away from it.

"Sit down and make yourselves comfortable, bitches," Trick sneered as he shoved Lacey and me toward the chairs.

The four men stepped in closer as we sat down, and they looked at us as if we were their prey. Trick came up and began to pace back and forth, folding his arms over his chest. "Before my shit-bag son gets here with his Reaper Bastard faggots, me and my brothers here are gonna make our own porn film with the both of you. Which cunt wants to go first?"

As the men turned and walked toward the mattress, I feared that both Lacey and I might not survive what was about to happen to us.

"Please don't hurt Dani! She's pregnant!" Lacey cried out, standing from the chair. "Take me, but please don't kill me!"

Trick looked at me and started to laugh. "Well, isn't that fan-fucking-tastic!" He was quick, snatching Lacey by the arm.

I was out of my chair, falling to my knees at Trick's feet.
"No! Please, Trick! I'm begging you! Please don't do this!"

Trick backhanded me across my face.

The whole world was spinning.

Lacey screamed and screamed again.

Men's laughter.

I tried to pull myself up off the ground.

Then I heard nothing. I saw nothing. Only blackness.

CHAPTER 20
HEAVY

REAPER BASTARDS

 MC

WASHINGTON, D.C.

Trick said noon, but I didn't give a fuck. The prospect drove my truck that Dani left parked at Lacey's house, and I led the Reaper Bastards at full throttle down the interstate and pulled up to the Bloody Aces clubhouse at eleven a.m.

As we all climbed off the bikes, Trick sauntered out the side door. His belt was unbuckled, and he wiped some blood off his hands with a dirty rag. Was that Dani's blood or Lacey's?

"Bring the girls out now, motherfucker!" I snarled at him, ready to bash my fists into him.

Trick dropped the bloody rag on the ground when four more Bloody Aces came walking out the side door. "I know your little bitch is knocked up, so I've changed my mind. I lost a hundred grand seven years ago since you let her get away. Then the other one ended up fucking dead! I lost my money, my patch, and my fucking club. And my own flesh and blood took it all from me!"

Trick shrugged off his cut, and I did the same, handing it to Wrecker. I paced back and forth, cracking my knuckles, and stretched my neck side to side, ready to rip his throat out with my bare fuckin' hands.

Then I let my soon-to-be-dead father say his last words. "I'm taking everything from you now, son. The girl and the kid she's carrying belong to me. That stupid bitch with the fake tits is dead after we're done fuckin' her."

Trick raised his fists, but as I came at him, Roadkill grabbed my arm. "Don't kill. Just take him down. He's mine."

He released his grip on my arm, and I rushed and swung first, landing a hook to his jaw. He staggered back and came at me with a jab to my left eye. I heard a scream from inside the clubhouse, then Roadkill howled like a beast in pain as he ran into the clubhouse. The Bloody Aces were outnumbered against the Reaper Bastards and it became a bloody fight to the death with knives.

I was quicker than Trick as I moved around him and away from his reach. We circled each other a few more times, trading punches. Trick was slowing down and breathing harder than I was. I roared, colliding with him, and we fell to the ground. I was quick and moved my body over his. I slammed a fist into him repeatedly while keeping a tight grip on his throat, holding him in place.

It was over in the next few minutes after I knocked Trick out cold. I looked around and saw four Bloody Aces were covered in blood as they lay dead on the ground. The Reaper Bastards were sweating and catching their breaths while they wiped their bloody blades off on their bodies.

I ran inside the clubhouse and found Dani lying facedown on a dirty cement floor. I dropped to my knees and gently turned her over.

"Dani!" I shouted my voice cracking, and pulled her into my arms.

Her eyes fluttered open.

"Heavy. Please save Lacey," she whispered.

I looked up just then to see Roadkill walking toward me, while he carried Lacey wrapped in a dirty blanket. "They're both alive."

I picked Dani up and into my arms and carried her out of the clubhouse with Roadkill.

CHAPTER 21
DANI

REAPER BASTARDS

MC

WASHINGTON, D.C.

Heavy came with me for my sonogram appointment with Dr. Heller, and with DNA testing, we found out our baby was a little girl. Dr. Heller showed her to us on the monitor that looked like a TV screen. Our baby girl looked like a little tiny peanut, and Dr. Heller said she appeared normal and healthy. She was perfect to her mom and dad. I thought it would've been Heavy's worst nightmare come true since he was all freaked out if the baby was a girl, but his reaction was a big grin from ear to ear. He told me he was the happiest man on the planet.

Heavy saved my life again that day he carried me out of that warehouse. Roadkill was Lacey's knight in shining armor. Using his bare hands, he killed the man who was raping her on that mattress. Then Roadkill covered her naked body with a dirty blanket and carried her out of that clubhouse of horrors.

Roadkill wanted to take Lacey to the nearest hospital, but she refused to go and wanted to see her own doctor. The prospect, Teddy, drove us to Dr. Heller's office in Heavy's truck as the Reaper Bastards followed behind on their bikes. When we parked the truck, Roadkill carried Lacey into Dr. Heller's office.

I cried for days afterward, feeling so bad for all the pain Lacey had suffered from the gang rape. I knew she would recover physically, but she would always feel broken and never heal on the inside. Just like me. The pain and rage I saw in Roadkill's eyes was gut-wrenching too. Once Dr. Heller cleaned her wounds as best as she could, she prescribed some medications and pain killers for Lacey, advising her to come back again in the next few days. We drove Lacey home, and Roadkill stayed with her for weeks and slept on her couch.

Wrecker and Bagger stayed behind at the Bloody Aces clubhouse and loaded the dead bodies into that rusty van. Heavy didn't tell me everything that happened the day after, so I didn't know what they did with the bodies.

Heavy did, however, give me some gruesome details of what Roadkill had done to Trick. He was dragged into that clubhouse and regained consciousness. Then his wrists were stung up above him. How? I'm not really sure, but I did *not* ask. Roadkill kept a spare set of surgical instruments in the saddlebag on his bike. He used those instruments on Trick's body, slicing him open from the sternum to his balls while he was still alive.

EPILOGUE
DANI

REAPER BASTARDS

MC

WASHINGTON, D.C.

It was a hot and humid summer afternoon when I shopped in the fresh, cool air inside the grocery store. Sweat dripped down the crack between my tits while I loaded the bags of groceries into the passenger seat of the truck. I shut the door and walked around to the driver's side, and I jumped when I almost collided face-first with a woman standing behind the truck.

"I'm so sorry! I didn't mean to scare you!" she said as we both pressed a hand on our chests.

I laughed. "That's okay. We scared each other."

The woman looked to be in her mid-fifties with brown hair, and her eyes were dark gray, which reminded me of someone I felt I knew.

I offered her my hand. "Hi, I'm Dani."

She shook my hand. "Hello. I'm Sheila."

I held onto her hand. "Sheila? Sheila Stone?" Her name suddenly registered to my brain. "You're Heavy's mother! Uh. I mean, Hendrix is your son!"

"Yes. I found out through a friend of a friend sort of thing that his father, Patrick, is dead." Tears welled up in her eyes. "I know Hendrix hates me, and I don't want him to know I came back. I just...well, I just wanted to see him."

"But Sheila, he does *not* hate you! He's always had hope that you're still alive and happy!"

She smiled and sniffled. "Really?"

"Yes! Well, you just *have* to come see him now!" I placed her hand on my belly and began to cry tears of happiness. "Because you're going to be a grandmother."

THE END

About Linny Lawless

Linny grew up, lived, and worked in the Northern Virginia area, close to Washington, DC. She's a bookworm, biker chick, and international best-selling indie author. Linny published her debut novel, "Salvation in Chaos," in January 2018, and she's very passionate about writing suspenseful and action-packed stories. If Linny is not busy traveling, working, and writing, she spends her days at home in Front Royal, Virginia, with her husband, Norman, and 2 Brussel Griffons named Verdy and Simon.

Website:
https://linnylawless.com/

Made in the USA
Middletown, DE
06 September 2024

60512133R00066